Books by Ralph McInerny

Leave of Absence   1986
The Noonday Devil   1985
Connolly's Life   1983
Romanesque   1978
Spinnaker   1977
Rogerson at Bay   1976
Gate of Heaven   1975
The Priest   1973
A Narrow Time   1969
Jolly Rogerson   1967

THE FATHER DOWLING MYSTERY SERIES

Rest in Pieces   1985
Getting A Way with Murder   1984
The Grass Widow   1983
A Loss of Patients   1982
Thicker Than Water   1981
Second Vespers   1980
Lying Three   1979
Bishop as Pawn   1978
The Seventh Station   1977
Her Death of Cold   1976

Leave of Absence

RALPH MC INERNY

Leave of Absence

Atheneum   NEW YORK   *1986*

Fiction Catalog 12th ed

Library of Congress Cataloging-in-Publication Data

McInerny, Ralph M.
    Leave of absence.

    I. Title.
PS3563.A31166L39   1986   813'.54   85-48150
ISBN 0-689-11783-3

Published simultaneously in Canada by Collier Macmillan Canada, Inc.
Composition by Maryland Linotype Composition Company
Baltimore, Maryland
Manufactured by Haddon Craftsmen, Scranton, Pennsylvania
Designed by Harry Ford
First Edition

For Ceil *and* Austin

L'arte nasce dallo stupore
di fronte alla sacralita della vita.

Contents

PART ONE

Another Country

I.

Sixteen years to the day after she married Edward—she no longer thought of it as an anniversary—Vera came out of the Hotel Columbus on the Via della Conciliazione, turned to her left, and walked toward St. Peter's.

She wore a raincoat and carried an umbrella, but her prematurely gray hair was uncovered to the misty rain. Her hair was her comfort if not her glory, thick, with a natural wave, nothing exaggerated. It was the one thing about herself she had never wished to change.

She passed by places featuring trinkets for tourists, *oggetti religiosi* in the worst possible taste—a crucified Jesus opened and shut his eyes as she went by—under a final archway, and into the great round square of St. Peter.

Round Square. Squaring the circle. Hadn't that always been the favored example of illogical effort? The wet cobbled pavement tried to reflect mosaically the massive basilica embraced by Bernini's colonnades, a Renaissance comment on the ancient obelisk in the piazza, whose two great flanking fountains splashed on in the rain.

Vera came to a stop in the all but deserted square to let the place exert its power. It was her third day in

Rome, her half-specious purpose in coming delayed
until today, when she would meet Katy for lunch. On
the phone last night her niece had sounded like anything but the dangerously depressed girl Dolores had
bitten her lower lip in talking about. But then Katy
had pretended she did not know her aunt would be in
Rome.

"How long are you here for?"

"Your mother insisted I call you." Stupid remark,
unthinkingly made. "Can we have lunch?"

"On you?"

"On me."

Vera carefully wrote down directions to the *trattoria*
selected by Katy because of its proximity to her aunt's
hotel.

Standing now in St. Peter's square, Vera did not feel
the appropriate emissary to disentangle Katy from whatever emotional net she was caught in. Out in the rain
in the middle of Christendom, thinking of her own
failed marriage, Vera had the sense of being a lost soul
if there ever was one.

High above the square was the window of the pontif-
ical palace from which the pope spoke to the assembled
faithful, and the world, each Sunday at noon. The
Angelus. Vera had easily followed his amplified Italian
as she peered up at him from the crowd. How sure he
seemed, rocklike, a stranger to doubt. Looking out over
the very square in which he had been shot, he yet con-
veyed a smiling Slavic certainty that all would be well.

That is how I felt once, Vera thought. As a wife if
not as a lawyer. She had not doubted that being Edward's wife was a role she would occupy until death. Ha.

She glared now at the pope's window as if it were he, not Edward, who had let her down. In the rain the dampness on her face felt like tears because, at least in part, it was. An unsought effect of this trip was such sudden bouts of self-pity. She actually felt sorry for herself! The one emotion she had always despised in others now revealed its seductive charm. She had always been Vera the strong. Superwoman. Her enemies said Edward had found another mother in her, her friends said she had introduced order and stability into his life.

Had Edward viewed Andrea as mother or organizer? Or was it neither that he wanted?

The rain was harder now, and she put up her umbrella as if to stop her tears as well and set off toward the wide, ramplike steps of the basilica.

On her way to Mass. What a church mouse she had become.

She felt almost like a nun.

A nun. That was not even remotely funny.

The Goodyear blimp could have sailed about inside the Basilica of St. Peter. Entering it was no more confining than leaving it, and Vera needed some niche or chapel to feel truly indoors—though even the side chapels had the dimensions of normal churches. Everywhere in the vast basilica, priests were saying Masses. They emerged all vested from the sacristy carrying covered chalices and following laconic acolytes, beautiful Italian boys in pre-puberty for the most part, done up like little priests themselves in red cassocks and white surplices, a missal under one arm and the cruets of wine and water swinging from the hand of the other.

Did they just hunt up a deserted altar or lead their priests to assigned spots? Vera wondered what non-Catholic tourists made of it all. She wasn't sure what she made of it all herself. Especially the confessionals.

In ambulatories, nestled against pillars, standing in rows in the transept, unobstrusive yet everywhere, were the confessionals, a priest visible behind a little Dutch door, on either side of him places for penitents to kneel as they confessed their sins through the grille. It was hard not to stare.

How long had it been since she had gone to confession? She found that she couldn't remember. Everything was different now, the rules and practices of her girlhood fallen into disuse. Then she had confessed every two weeks; a month was a dangerously long interval. Gradually—when exactly?—things had changed. There was talk of reconciliation rather than penance, with the suggestion that soon there would be general absolution given to all as to soldiers going into battle. Once, Andrea, lifelong friend, expert in such matters, had solemnly assured her that the confession of sins at the beginning of Mass—now become the Eucharistic Celebration—more than sufficed. No need to go groveling to the priest.

In those days Andrea's authority in religious questions was unequivocal. Andrea was still the strictest of Catholics then.

2.

Compared with the constantly roiled waters of her sister Dolores's life, Vera's had always seemed a pacific ocean. Overweight, her hair a mess, her attention span somewhere around two minutes, Dolores nonetheless held her hectic household more or less together. Howard drank too much, no longer even pretending to discipline the kids, sat flaked out in front of the television till all hours. Televisions. He used two sets, each equipped with a remote control, the better to watch fragments of every sporting event on the tube. Any energy he had was used up in his daytime efforts as a manufacturer's representative.

"Salesman," Dolores explained.

"Don't knock it, honey." Howard was not irked.

Was Dolores? She quoted her now supine spouse. " 'Salesmen built this country.' "

Apparently that was one of the tenets of Howard's creed. And creed was the right word. Jesus had been a salesman, too, the best there ever was.

Once Vera had felt condescending toward her sister and Howard and a little bit sorry for their kids, but after her own life fell apart, she would sit drinking coffee with Dolores as if somewhere in her sister's life were concealed a secret she should have learned herself. For a while there Vera was prepared to believe that everyone but she knew the secret of life. Dolores was wearing a jogging outfit when she brought up the subject of her youngest daughter.

"I'm worried about Katy."

"What's wrong?"

"I wish I knew."

Katy, the youngest of Dolores's five daughters, was spending her junior year abroad, in Rome.

"What does she say?"

"Nothing. She never writes, of course, but twice on the phone she started crying and couldn't tell me why."

"How is she doing in her classes?"

"Classes." Dolores made a face. "She got a pink slip at midsemester. In mythology. I thought that was the explanation, but I doubt it. Katy's smart enough. If she's having trouble in class, it's something else. I have half a mind to get on a plane and find out what's going on."

"Are you really worried?"

"Me worry?" Dolores crossed her eyes and assumed an idiotic Alfred E. Neuman grin.

That had been the origin of Vera's trip to Rome, Katy's real or imagined problems her excuse for going. She requested a leave of absence from the law firm and had to insist when Patterson, the eponymous senior partner, tried to talk her out of it.

"Work is the only answer, Vera." He said this after nodding silently for a full minute, his lips pursed, concern rippling his forehead.

And what was the question? "I've thought it through, Mr. Patterson. If you insist, I will resign from the firm."

"No, no. Take a vacation. A long vacation. But put a time limit on it, Vera. My advice isn't entirely selfish.

Of course we will miss you while you're gone. You already know that. But indolence can become a habit. I've seen it happen. You yourself have seen the things people think they want to do after a divorce. It's all perfectly understandable."

This did not annoy her as much as it might have. It helped that he acknowledged her importance to the firm. That should have influenced her, even changed her mind; she could not understand why it did not. Why wasn't it enough to know she was indispensable to the smooth operation of Patterson, Patterson, Flood and Barrett? She had specialized in computer law, presided over the computerization of the office, experienced the hieratic power of one who knows what others do not. Patterson senior still had misgivings about the electric typewriter, let alone computers. But Vera had carried the day against this Luddite attitude and become indispensable to the firm in the process.

She took her leave of absence. She all but cleared out her office, wondering if she ever would return to it. Indolence can become a habit. So can thought. The kind of thought she had been engaging in since Edward first told her he wanted a divorce.

What does it all mean?

The practice of law does not lend itself to pondering such questions. Vera had the sense that she was becoming a child again, yet growing wise as well. Well, not wise. But she wanted to be wise, she wanted to know why it made the least bit of difference whether she did a thing or its opposite. She felt that she was returning to the dreams of her youth. Her undergraduate major had been philosophy—always a good pre-law major, that was the advice she had gotten, but she'd become mildly hooked on it. Not the recent stuff—logical games, linguistic questions, a sort of debating club atmosphere— but things like Plato. The *Apology* of Socrates. The unexamined life is not worth living. Now, all these years later, she was half-ashamed at the return of undergraduate enthusiasm, but such reading seemed the one pleasure she had. Her improbable meditations could only profit from a complete change of scene.

"Dolores, I'll go."

"Don't be silly. I can't ask you to do a thing like that. Besides, you'd be too easy on Katy."

"You're hard?"

"She thinks so."

"Because you let her spend a year in Europe?"

"From Rome she calls me up to cry! I've never been to Europe in my life."

Vera surprised herself by suggesting they go together. Dolores's glasses had slid down her nose; she had made a single tube of the joined sleeves of her jogging costume, concealing her hands. She tipped her head to one side and just looked at Vera. It was a dumb idea.

"Then I'll go alone."

"Sure."

"Dolores, I want to go. And I will."

So her niece's unexplained weeping on the transatlantic phone was the explanation for Vera's trip. It made it sound almost tax-deductible. Would she have come to Europe without Katy as an excuse? This went beyond indolence to escape. And as Patterson senior would have pointed out, she was the very cliché of the new divorcée, off to see the world with a vague glint in her eye, half-dreading that she might have an adventure. Adventure! It turned out to be more of a retreat, in the religious sense. A withdrawal in order to think about her life and wonder what next.

3.

The fact that she had really and truly been surprised when Edward told her he wanted a divorce had come to seem a serious flaw in her character. Nearly two years had passed since the awful day. Her first impulse had been to laugh—dutifully; as she did when Howard referred to Dolores as his first wife. But she soon realized that laughter was not in order. Edward's seriousness had turned the husband she no longer took seriously into a stranger. It was like seeing a sudden, unexpected reflection of herself and thinking it was someone she could never like. Edward, at thirty-seven, was as familiar to her as herself, tall, with a weak mouth, eyes that could not meet hers. He had the soul of a dentist. The fact that he was smoking a cigarette when he told her had provided a welcome diversion.

"Put it out. You'll get hooked again."

"I never really quit, Vera."

"Of course you quit."

"I've been smoking all along." His voice lifted in anger.

She couldn't believe it. "But when? At the office?"

"Whenever I could sneak the damned things. A quick smoke, then a lozenge. God. I couldn't admit to you I hadn't quit."

She had considered his addiction to breath fresheners an occupational hazard. It would not do to breathe bad breath into a patient's face while urging dental hygiene.

"And now you can?"

His smile was like a schoolboy's. "That's right! Now it doesn't matter."

"Edward, you don't have to get a divorce in order to smoke cigarettes. Smoke if you want to. I was concerned for your health." She let her voice dwindle away as she noticed its motherly tone.

"It's not just cigarettes."

"Where there's smoke?"

Such kidding had always gotten them through the rare rough spots their marriage had known. Had they ever had a serious argument? Maybe they should have. Howard and Dolores engaged in a constant exchange of verbal sniping that seemed part of their bond. Vera felt she had betrayed her Italian blood—one-quarter, on her mother's side. She was not meant to be so damned calm and rational. But Edward had always leaned on her. If she felt indispensable to Patterson, Patterson, Flood and Barrett, she felt even more indispensable to Edward. What would he do without her? Without someone to prop him up?

Vera asked who the other woman was, wanting to scream at the soap operaish scenario. Did she really care? It was Edward who had betrayed her, not some woman. At least he claimed he had. She could not believe he

meant to leave her because she could not really believe
he had been unfaithful.

"Edward, you're thirty-seven years old."

"I know!"

She might have hit upon his motive. He became
almost eloquent, trite phrases tripping from his tongue.
His life was drifting away. He was unhappy. He had to
act before it was too late.

He added, trying to alter his anguished expression of
self-pity, "And I know I make you unhappy, Vera."

That was phony, of course. Happy, unhappy—what
did that have to do with marriage? Marriage was forever. They were Catholics. There was no point in divorce; he couldn't marry again anyway, not really. Did
he intend to live the rest of his life in sin?

He stared at her as if she had invented their religion.
"We can't get an annulment," he said bleakly.

"An annulment!"

"I thought because we had never had any kids . . ."

That had been the unkindest cut of all, worse than
the initial revelation, far worse. Apparently he had
consulted a priest about the chances of annulment and
had been discouraged.

"You actually talked to a priest about our marriage?"

"I got an opinion, yes."

He lit another cigarette, and it occurred to her that
she was making this easy for him. But it would have
been difficult to throw a tantrum in the restaurant
where this incredible conversation was taking place.

"Let's have lunch," he'd said. She'd been pleased by
his suggestion and had agreed that the Loop was
impossible.

"Let's meet at one of the suburban malls."

Only in retrospect was she struck by how knowledgeable he had sounded. So there they sat, among the suburban matrons of Skokie, drinking the mandatory Chablis, discussing the end of her life.

4.

"Bless me, Father, for I have sinned."

The old words came easily after she had eased herself onto the uncomfortable wooden kneeler and the confessional grille had slid open.

"Yes."

She had walked by this confessional several times, peeking at the priest, thinking it wouldn't be so bad to kneel there and tell all about herself. The sign above the confessional's door indicated that he heard sins in English and French as well as Italian. Exotic. Strange. She could kneel there and confess everything, and it would be both real and unreal. But having knelt and said the correct opening phrases, she could not remember what to do next.

"How long has it been since your last confession?"

"I have no idea, Father. I just stopped going, years ago. Nobody seemed to go anymore . . ."

"You're from New York, aren't you?" A lilt in his voice.

"No, Father. Chicago."

"You're serious?"

"Yes." It seemed an inauspicious beginning. Did he

pride himself on recognizing regional accents? Vera felt even more of an impostor now.

He chuckled. "You wouldn't lie in the confessional, would you? I was sure I detected a New York accent."

"Are you from New York?"

"That's right. And *from* is the right word. I've been in Rome most of my life."

"Here at St. Peter's?" She had the image of him imprisoned in this confessional as the years went by, his life drifting away like Edward's.

He found her remark funny. He actually laughed. This was not at all as she had supposed it would be, and she wasn't sure she liked it.

"So they convinced you confession wasn't necessary anymore, did they?"

"I don't want to blame anyone else."

"There are false teachers, my child. False teachers. Here in Rome we have the great blessing to have the Holy Father teaching us. A great man. A holy man. You listen to him and tell me nothing's the same, everything's changed. Not a bit of it." He seemed to stop himself from going on with a familiar homily. "Are you married?"

"No." She inhaled. "Not anymore."

"Ah."

"I'm divorced."

She could make out his face easily now and saw him wince at the mention of divorce.

"Have you taken another man?" He made it sound nasty.

"Father, my husband left me. *He* divorced *me*. It was his idea, not mine. He *left* me."

She spoke with sudden fury, aware of a tour group passing the confessional. Or were they surrounding it? Vera felt caught up in a mild melodrama, a passing curiosity to Japanese tourists, but at the same time she wanted this confession to take.

"You've remained unmarried since your husband left you?"

"Yes." Did he regard it as an accomplishment? What stories he must listen to, sitting here day after day. Perhaps he had reason to think people fell into bed or marriage at the least provocation. It seemed almost a confessable fault that she had not been pursued at all since having, in the phrase, regained her freedom. "Father, I didn't come here to blame other people. I want to confess my sins."

"Very well. Begin."

"Help me."

So he went down a list for her, and she tried to accuse herself of lack of charity, of vanity, of anger and greed, and of all the deadly sins, but that would have seemed braggadocio. It was a depressing thought that she was neither good nor bad.

"Have you been attending Mass on Sundays?"

"Lately, yes."

"There were times when you did not?"

There had been years when she did not. At the beginning of their life together, she and Edward had gone dutifully to Sunday Mass. They had been particularly devout when children had not come, hoping to pray their way to fertility. It had not worked, but they had kept on asking long after she suspected that Edward was not as saddened as he pretended by her barrenness.

16

Except that she was not barren. She refused to take tests when Edward suggested them, fearing a definitive negative judgment, but eventually, without telling him, she did, and a doctor who looked like a college freshman assured her there was nothing wrong with her.

"But I've been married four years and I'm still not pregnant."

He started to say something but thought better of it. Her expression might have warned him. She would have slapped him if he'd said they needed sex instruction.

"It must be your husband."

She could not have told Edward that, not ever. It would have been too cruel. She knew that because of her own relief on learning she was able to have children. Dolores thought they were practicing birth control. All this talk about not being able to bear children was nonsense. She brushed the hair from her forehead with the back of her forearm. As far as Dolores was concerned, getting pregnant was the easiest thing in the world.

"I can do it lying down."

Vera did not want to think of Dolores in bed with Howard. For her, sex had become what she and Edward had to do if they were to have a child. Had it become a duty for Edward, too? Maybe if they just relaxed and enjoyed themselves . . . So she surprised him with a Caribbean vacation, making all the arrangements herself—that is, having Teresa, the girl who handled travel for the firm, do it.

"A vacation?" Edward loved surprises, and this was out of the ordinary. "Where?"

She moved close against him. "The Virgin Islands."

It hadn't worked. The young doctor must have guessed correctly. She never told Edward he was the reason they had no children, even accepted his unstated implication that the deficiency was hers.

She had kept her silence even during the awful lunch in Skokie when he told her he wanted a divorce. It would have seemed a vengeful cruelty to mention it then. He would have dismissed it as a lie told to protect herself. Not that Edward had any interest in children now.

Even if Andrea had been able to bear children, nature would soon render her naturally barren.

The priest on the other side of the grille began to tell her the Gospel story of the woman who had been ill for years and then was cured when she touched the hem of Jesus' garment.

"We're not told explicitly, but it seems clear the woman had been menstruating continuously for years. A dreadful ailment. But all she did was touch Jesus' garment and she was cured. That is what we do when we come to confession, touch the hem of Jesus' garment and the power goes out from him and we are healed."

She might have been receiving counsel at an intersection in downtown Chicago. There a ceaseless traffic of tourists and worshipers and priests being led to and fro by acolytes all around the confessional. Somehow the surrealistic circumstances made it easier to be kneeling there. Before giving her absolution, the priest hold her to say the rosary as penance.

"Do you have a rosary?"

"I'll get one."

"You should say the rosary every day. How old are you?"

The question shocked her. "What difference does it make?"

"You needn't tell me if you don't want to."

"I am thirty-seven years old." He could not absolve her of that.

"Consider this. Your life may be half over. You may have less time yet to live than you've lived already. Any of us could die at any minute. Why did God make you?"

The catechism answer formed in her head, and she smiled. "God made me to know him, to love him and to serve him in this world and to be happy with him forever in the next."

"Good. And don't ever forget it."

After she had received absolution, Vera got to her feet and wandered into the nave. She was drifting toward the main door when she was distracted by the altar of the Blessed Sacrament and decided to sit awhile in the side chapel to think about what she had just done.

Reflection on her life had attracted her ever since Edward had moved out and imposed on her the need to think of what her future would be. She could go on practicing law, of course. That was her profession and thank God for it. She neither needed nor wanted anything from Edward. Dolores had proved surprisingly vindictive on that point.

"You should go for everything the bastard has."

"What good would it do?"

"I was thinking of the harm."

Maybe she herself thought it would be more punitive to ask Edward for nothing. She could support herself. She always had, really; her contribution to the household had been almost as great as Edward's. She could hardly equal his income, of course, dentistry being a license to steal.

But knowing she could work did not tell her how she would live.

The catechism answer that had popped into her head in the confessional was the sort of thought she wanted to sum up her life. What did the practice of law have to do with knowing, loving, and serving God? Rome seemed a good place to think about that, and if she could be of some help to Katy besides, so much the better.

As for herself, she was on a retreat. She wanted to know the meaning of life. She wanted to figure out what she would do, and why, with whatever time remained to her. And, as she had not dreamed of doing for years, she meant to consult God about it.

5.

She arrived at the Trattoria da Giulio at the end of an aimless walk from the Vatican in the direction of the Piazza Cavour. Rain came and went, and in between the sun appeared with all the brightness of false hope. During one brief shower Vera stepped into a shop to buy the rosary on which to say her penance.

Beads ranged from quite expensive jewelry items, through the gaudy, to the merely serviceable. Paying a lot might have seemed to add to the penance, but Vera selected the cheapest rosary, black beads strung on thin wire, the body on the crucifix amorphous.

The clerk, bejeaned, big-bottomed, spike-heeled, turned off her charm and wrapped the rosary in a little square of paper.

Under advisement Vera wore her purse with the strap across her body. There had even been the suggestion that she button it under her coat, but being robbed seemed preferable to such precaution. Besides, she felt she was as likely to be robbed in shops as on the street.

Using the Castel Sant'Angelo as her reference point, Vera followed the outer wall of the Vatican to a large square, where buses and streetcars and taxis predominated, and then went along the Via Cola di Rienzo. Her map told her she should turn right at the Via Tacito. Tacito? Tacit? But the neighboring streets—Boezio, Virgilio, Orazio, and Cicerone—gave the clue. Tacitus, the historian. What had she read of him in school? Something on Germany, but he was famous for his history of Rome. Or was that Livy?

Maybe she had not misunderstood the name. There is a tacit history as well as the history of Tacitus. The untold, unrecorded deeds of the mass of mankind, too insignificant to be named in the chronicles of greatness. This very street was filled with people no historian would notice, yet each person's life was of infinite importance, to him- or herself, if not to Tacitus. Careening traffic in the street, an unending flow of people in both directions, some in a hurry, some not, others obviously just out to take a look at the world, domestic tourists as well as her kind. Business, the necessities of life, sex. `*`

Even women of an age carried themselves with a consciousness of being desirable, and it was the rare male eye that did not cast an appraising glance at every passing female. Despite herself, Vera was vaguely flattered at the attention she received. Her purse? Nonsense. Someone should do something about the almost hysterical warnings given the traveler to Italy. One's virtue was in more danger than one's supply of traveler's checks.

A cappuccino in a café, several spoonsful of sugar, such insouciance underlining the fact that she was on vacation. On leave of absence. She drank her coffee standing at the bar like everyone else, no longer surprised at her ability to negotiate in Italian.

In school she had studied it as a kind of lark, but also in deference to the one-quarter of her blood that was Italian. "*Cappuccio,*" called the woman at the *cassa* where Vera bought the ticket to present at the bar. As the boy filled what looked like an ice cream scoop with coffee and fitted it onto the espresso machine, Vear made a mental note. Apparently it was effete not to use the diminutive. Her Italian was largely literary, Manzoni, of course—she had plowed dutifully through *I Promessi Sposi*—but also Pirandello. Dante and Petrarch only in dribs and drabs. She meant to turn Italian into a usable instrument during this stay.

Why? Just because, that's why.

A suit in a window caught her eye, and she spent twenty-five minutes managing not to buy it or anything else. She tried on the suit, thus raising the expectations

22

of the patrician proprietress, who looked as if she belonged in a palazzo rather than this modest store. Vera
was finally allowed to leave, a malevolent smile following her into the street.

She had started out with the idea that she had more
than enough time to keep her appointment with Katy,
but she ended by hurrying up the Via Tacito. The
number of *trattorie*, *hostarie*, and *ristoranti* discon-
certed her, and she began to think it might be a problem to find Da Giulio.

Vera arrived five minutes before the appointed time.
"*Due persone*," she said when she entered the small
restaurant, where only three people were already eating.
The owner wore a gorgeous sweater. He was lean as a
boy, and the glint in his eye did not entirely go away
when he realized she was not alone. He looked beyond
her quizzically, and she explained that her niece would
be joining her.

"*La sua nipote*," he cried, the glint back in full force.
Vera wondered if she had unwittingly entered into
some pact with him. Why had she mentioned it was her
niece who would be joining her? Idiotic.

She followed him to her seat, allowed mineral water
and bread to be brought, then waited.

Fifteen minutes later Katy showed up, and by that
time there was scarcely an empty table. The sound of
voices, the clink of tableware, the sensuous pleasure
taken in the act of eating, had altered the ambience of
the place.

The first thing to be said about Katy was that she had
no sense of clothes. The second, that it did not matter.

She had youth instead, a round-cheeked face in cheerful complicity with her eyes and mouth even when she was not smiling. Vera had vivid memories of her niece as a baby, but Katy was undoubtedly a young woman now, despite the jeans, the baggy sweater, and an unsuccessful attempt to neutralize her strawberry blonde hair through insufficient washing and a god-awful arrangement.

Dubious at first, the smiling proprietor led Katy between rows of little tables toward her waving aunt. Vera decided against rising, wedged as she was against the wall. Standing, they might have embraced; seated, Vera took her niece's hand, half expecting Katy to kiss hers in return.

"I can't get up."

"You're looking good," Katy cried, pulling out the chair opposite Vera and beginning to squirm out of her knapsack. With smiles and an Italian effusion Vera could not follow, the owner urged her into another chair. He did not want Katy blocking that narrow aisle between the tables. So they ended up sitting at right angles, with Katy peering at her aunt with a half smile. "I mean it. You do look good."

"You sound surprised."

"I guess I am. A little."

"Katy, it's all over now and I have accepted it and I will be just fine."

"You came to Europe all alone?"

Katy spoke of Europe with a proprietary air; after a few months on it, she owned the continent. Vera had felt the same way after her own first visit.

"Your mother wanted to come, but she finally decided she couldn't afford it. And she wouldn't let me help her."

"She didn't really want to come."

"Don't kid yourself. She's worried about you."

"So she sent you?"

"I was coming anyway."

Katy took a package of cigarettes from her knapsack. An Italian brand. Vera forced herself not to say anything. Had Katy smoked at home? It was unbelievable to her that anyone would start smoking now, knowing what we know about cigarettes. Having exhaled a huge cloud of smoke, Katy waved her hand a few times, as if to clear the air.

"And so you're here."

"What's wrong, Katy?" Best to plunge right in before Katy established an invulnerable persona.

"Does something have to be wrong?"

"No, but it would help. Don't tell me I came all this way for nothing."

"So you really did come just to see me."

Vera shook her head. "You were just my excuse."

"Good. I don't mind that."

But after a glass of wine, Katy's tongue was loosened. Vera refilled her glass with the feeling that she was corrupting youth. The problem, of course, was a boy. A young man. A seminarian.

"At the North American College," Katy added, as if that explained it.

Vera wondered if she had come all this way to learn that her niece was in love with a boy who intended to

Leave of Absence

live a celibate life. But if Katy's story was true, it was
difficult to blame her for getting involved with Kenneth.

"Kenneth Stewart. They had a reception and I met
him there and we began to go out."

"On dates?"

"To movies in Trastevere. Out to eat."

"Just the two of you?"

More often than not with others, but they were
together, Katy and Kenneth, they knew it, everyone
knew it.

"Including the North American College?"

Katy frowned. "How do you mean?"

"Does he intend to become a priest?"

"That's why he's here."

"Why does he want to be a priest?"

Katy had never asked him. It was obvious she thought
of him as she might any boy with whom she had fallen
in love. Seminarians out on dates? Vera realized she was
not really shocked. It seemed a small addendum to the
general confusion and disarray. The theory was that
young men should be sure they could say no to married
life before they assumed the obligation of celibacy. Obviously a male idea. The theory did not account for the
girls who would be the objects of the experiments. Perhaps Katy believed celibacy would stop being a condition of ordination.

"Whatever the future brings, Katy, priests can't marry
now."

"Marry! He doesn't know I exist, not really. He just
wants someone to talk to."

"We all need that."

26

Katy took the remark as an invitation to sympathize with her abandoned aunt. Vera was happy to get away from the subject of the seminarian. The whole problem reminded her of Andrea. Besides, there was a distraction at the next table, where a priest and two nuns had been seated.

His voice had struck Vera from the first time she heard it, and now she knew why. It was her confessor of that morning, she was sure of it. His thin hair was slicked back, and his glasses caught the light as he leaned toward one nun and then the other—impartial, that seemed to be the idea, impartial and condescending. He treated the two nuns, who looked to be in their late forties, as if they were children. The one with a pronounced overbite deferred to him shamelessly.

"Aren't those good beans, Father?"

He did not wait to swallow. "Know how they taste best?"

"Father?"

"I mean the ones you don't eat. Serve them cold with a little vinegar. Delicious."

Apparently he was an expert cook; for twenty minutes he instructed the nuns on what to buy and how to prepare it, speaking with consummate authority. His guests did everything but take notes. Vera, remembering him from the confessional, was thankful that the efficacy of the sacrament did not depend on her opinion of the confessor.

Katy said, "Why did you come to Rome in November? If I were you, I'd be in Athens."

"Maybe I'll go there next."

"Do you mean it?"

Vera smiled. It was pleasant to feel so footloose—Athens, Cairo, maybe Istanbul. Why not? After a rainy day in Rome, she might indeed be ready for it.

At the next table the priest was saying of someone that he was a traitor, he let us down. "I don't have any sympathy with him at all. Her? I don't know. She probably felt she could trust a priest."

"She knew what she was doing," the older nun said.

Vera tuned it out, sensing another proof that things were out of control, nothing was what it seemed, promises were made to be broken. It reduced things to the least common denominator to think that what Edward had done was fail to keep his word. But marriage was a contract, after all, odd as it seemed to make love a matter of law.

"You really ought to go to Athens, Aunt Vera."

"Come with me."

"I can't!" But there was the catch of doubt in her voice. Did she imagine dropping out of school and bumming around Europe with her divorced aunt? Vera half feared Katy would take her up on her facetious offer.

"Mom would kill me."

"Getting away might solve your problem."

"Does it?"

The clerical voice had dropped to a whisper. He might have been assigning the two nuns a penance.

"Travel *is* broadening."

"Don't I know it."

Katy had put on weight. The prospect of extra pounds did not frighten Vera.

"I can imagine what my mother would say if she knew I had a crush on a seminarian."

Vera laughed. "I think she would want to say it to the boy."

Katy smiled in response to the laugh, then pursed her lips and shook her head at her mother's imagined reaction.

"Mothers are sometimes right, Katy."

"Mine is always right."

"You're a very lucky girl."

"I was being sarcastic."

"So was I."

The Holy Time Is Quiet as a Nun

I.

Andrea was early drawn to the religious life and the prospect of making herself a living oblation. When the *Andrea Doria* sank in 1956, thoughts of shipwreck began to take on a metaphorical significance. After all, the Doria family invoked by the ship's name (and her own) had given a Pope to the Church. In high school she discovered Hopkins, and the priest poet's dedication to "The Wreck of the Deutschland" seemed somehow addressed to her:

To the happy memory of five Franciscan Nuns exiles by the Falk Laws drowned between midnight and morning of Dec. 7th, 1875

December seventh. Pearl Harbor.

It was much, much later that the suggestion of treachery and maidenly shipwreck dominated Andrea's notion of herself. Those poor, doomed nuns, drowned for the sake of the kingdom of heaven, stirred her soul. Youth is a time when we fairly lust after self-sacrifice.

Hopkins's dedication prompted her to inquire about the Franciscans, and she soon learned that Il Poverello's order had fragmented into a bewildering number of groups, the female branch even more than the male. What she eventually entered was one of the more obscure species of Franciscans, with a motherhouse in

Wisconsin, a liberal arts college for women in Green Bay, and several dozen parochial school assignments in Minnesota, Iowa, and northern Illinois. She could not have devised a more thorough rejection of the world and its criteria of importance.

A postulant at eighteen, she finished the novitiate the month before her twentieth birthday, in the year of Our Lord 1974. Took simple vows, and, less than two years after entering the convent, could scarcely remember her life outside. As a novice she had written only to her parents, but after vows the rule was less stringent, and Andrea, or Sister Duns Scotus, as she had become, wrote a letter to Vera Halloran, not realizing she was beginning what would become a voluminous correspondence. Vera had been her closest friend in the world. They confided everything to one another, seldom agreed about anything, yet clung together as if each of their personalities required its polar opposite in order to feel stable. Andrea was anxious to see if Vera could guess why she had chosen the religious name she had.

Vera's correct guess was expressed in a way that aroused the wary curiosity of the mother superior. On a postcard Vera typed only ". . . these walls are what He haunted who of all men most sways my spirits to peace."

Andrea brought the Peter Pauper edition of Hopkins's poems from the library and showed mother superior "Duns Scotus's Oxford." It never even occurred to her to question Mother Agnes's right to an explanation. She left the office with her superior's benediction and the renewed sense that she had chosen her religious name well. In her room, written on a three-by-five index card in her fine, nunnish hand, the final stanza of the poem was Scotch-taped to the wall over her desk.

Of reality the rarest-veined unraveller; a not
Rivalled insight, be rival Italy or Greece;
Who fired France for Mary without spot.

She took her degree from their own college, St. Clare, and was sent at twenty-two to Marquette to do graduate work in theology. It was only then she realized that by the Italian rival Hopkins meant Saint Thomas Aquinas.

Vera had gone to St. Catherine's, where she majored in philosophy and, unaware that there were other choices—like Andrea herself the beneficiary or victim of a time warp in which Vatican II had yet to be felt in all its fury—became a Thomist. As girls they had dreamed of becoming poets; they ended up smitten by theology and philosophy. Both claimed to see logic in what had happened. If Andrea could lay claim to Hopkins, Vera countered with Claudel. She had tried Dante at first, but Andrea had convinced her that Scotus as well as Aquinas had influenced the great Florentine. They traded the verses from the *Paradiso*. Dear God, what fun that had been, snug and comfortable within the cocoon of Catholic culture yet feeling in tune with what unabashedly they would call the Western Tradition.

Such exchanges came easily only in letters. On the few occasions when they met, there was the massive obstacle of Andrea's habit and the unignorable fact that they were embarked on wholly different paths. It was painfully obvious that Vera had not changed her mind

35

about the religious life. Not only did she not want it herself, she thought it a waste. That was an argument they no longer pursued even in letters.

It was not really a disagreement. The one girl did not have the other's vocation and vice versa, but that was like Vera's responding, "I don't," if Andrea said, "I have a headache." It went without saying that Vera wanted to become a wife and mother. When, after graduation, she went on to law school, Andrea felt a disapproval she thanked God later she had not expressed. On pure instinct Vera had chosen a course for which Andrea later would develop a theory. An ideology. Her later claim was that entering the convent had been an unconsciously feminist decision. She came to believe that. It gave her life the very continuity Vera claimed it lacked.

Boys. Andrea had gone on dates in high school, often doubling with Vera. She had danced and necked and once let a boy slide a trembling hand under her sweater and clumsily fondle her breast. It was like an experiment. She felt neither excitement nor revulsion. Not that she was in any danger. The boy had become so excited that he soon withdrew his hand, took her fiercely in his arms, and squirmed against her while making a mewling babylike sound.

"He was coming," Vera explained later.

Andrea smiled. Her Madonna smile. Would she have to mention this in confession?

Vera answered with a question. "Did you do anything?"

"You mean touch him?"

"No. Did anything happen to you?"

Andrea was not certain what she was denying. It was the kind of conversation she could not have with anyone but Vera. When girls alluded to their periods and cramps, invoking the sisterhood of pain and shame, Andrea escaped as soon as she could. The topic was meant to indicate maturity, being in touch with some deep female secret that excluded boys, but Andrea did not choose to take pride in something that happened to her body whether she liked it or not. Menstruation hardly seemed an accomplishment.

She wondered if anything had ever happened to Vera in such a situation, but she did not ask. It was not a topic she was keen on pursuing. The important lesson, for her at least, was that there was nothing about boys she could not live without. This was a disproof of Vera's unstated argument: that Andrea would change her mind when she met the right boy.

"Have you met the right boy?"

Vera did not have to think. "Of course not."

If Andrea's knowing smile could be called Madonna-like, Vera's was that of a wise old matron. The implication was that she would know, bells would ring, violins whine, the sun break through. Andrea did not mock her friend. She had already had a comparable epiphany when she thought about life in the convent.

Although she had not felt revulsion with that boy—his name was Arthur, but that did not matter; he had represented his whole sex—Andrea was aware of a reticence bordering on shame when, after gym classes, there was showering and nudity and a good deal of what seemed parading about the locker room on the part of her classmates. Not to want to appear naked before others was modesty, a virtue, not some mental quirk. Vera confessed to feeling the same uneasiness. It wasn't that they had not developed. Vera, though small, had a very full figure, and Andrea's height (she was five nine) did not disguise the fact that her breasts even then would have suggested to the literary Thackeray's description of Becky Sharp.

"Then how can you imagine being in bed with a boy?"

Vera's answer was a blush so deep it seemed to give her pain. Was this something Vera spent time imagining? A more dreadful thought occurred.

"Have you?"

"No!" Anger drove away the blush. "What a thing to say."

"Letting a boy see you naked would be far worse than being seen by another girl."

"Andrea, I don't imagine they just stand around and stare at one another. It isn't like that at all."

They had both tried without success to imagine their parents doing it. There was every reason to suppose they did, but this was like being sure there was a city named Paris that neither had ever seen. Conviction and experience were two different things. Had Vera spied as Andrea had, trying to overhear in the night the sounds of passion from her parents' room? There was far more likelihood that clues to sexual behavior would be picked up in visits to her older sister's house than at home, but Andrea had no better luck as a guest, though she did come upon the cardboard wheel containing her sister's pills.

"*The* pill," Charlotte said and, when she saw Andrea did not understand, explained that she and Willis did not want more children just yet. "There's nothing wrong with taking them," Charlotte insisted, as if she expected Andrea to object.

But Andrea was silenced by the implication of the pills. Charlotte and Bill slept together and . . . At this point a curtain fell across the stage of her imagination. It was good to go home and be free of such troubling speculation. Her parents, she decided, had stopped doing that sort of thing long ago. Her father was very nearly fifty, her mother just a few years younger. Andrea thought it absurd to imagine they were still making love like young people.

Her mother was predictably appalled when Andrea said she intended to become a nun. Her father, surprisingly, was not. His concern was less for her leaving the world than for the stories he had heard about convents.

"So many are leaving. There was that nun in St. Louis recently. Not that she looked like a nun." Her father smoked a pipe constantly, and his speech seemed as dependent on the pipe as music on an instrument.

Andrea assured him that the Franciscan community was very conservative. They dressed like nuns and they acted like nuns. The nun in Green Bay with whom she was corresponding had assured her that "they were implementing the directives of the council, the true directives, not its imagined spirit, which has led to such abuses." This seemed a reference to the defections and odd goings-on of which her father was so well informed.

"People get divorced," Andrea said in wild rebuttal.

39

Her mother, who was looking out the window, lower lip between her teeth, trying not to cry, swung around. "What do you mean?"

"The fact that some marriages break up is no argument against marriage, is it?"

"Why the Franciscans?" her father asked.

"My God," her mother cried. "Why the convent at all?"

"It's my vocation."

She loved that word and all it invoked: a divine plan that from all eternity had envisaged Andrea Bauer entering a convent in Green Bay, Wisconsin, where she would live her all too brief life in prayer and obscurity, growing closer and closer to God while interceding for others, particularly her loved ones.

"You would really lose me if I got married, Mom. Look at Charlotte."

"Charlotte is perfectly happy."

"I didn't say she wasn't."

"We're not losing a daughter, we're gaining a convent." Her father grinned around his pipe.

"Is Vera Halloran going, too?"

"No. Why would you think so?"

"This sounds like her idea."

Andrea laughed and put her arms around her mother. "Vera is the last person in the world who would enter the convent."

"She is a sensible girl. Andrea, go to college first, give it more thought. You need more experience of the world."

She had expected this. It was another version of the suggestion that all she had to do was meet the right man and she would change her mind. The convent was for old maids, women disappointed in love, misanthropes. She countered by telling her mother that the novitiate was a time of trial, to discover if she really wanted to be a nun, to see if the community wanted her.

"She could be back before we know it." But her father winked at Andrea as he said this.

Her mother went on about the parish convent, the modest building across the street from the church, where the nuns who taught in the parish school lived. On First Fridays and during Lent, Father Quinlan, the pastor, said the 6:45 Mass in the little convent chapel, sparing the nuns the trouble of trooping across the street and up the main aisle of the church to the two front pews on the Gospel side reserved for them. Andrea had attended those early morning Masses in the convent chapel with her mother, hurrying through frosty mornings, the cold air almost painful in the lungs, sniffling toward Bethlehem. Her mother's stride was stiff-legged and very fast. A babushka pulled over her head, her chin settled into the rabbit-fur collar of her chocolate-colored cloth coat, her mother seemed a living link to earlier no-nonsense generations extending back through time. A strong woman. *Mulier fortis.* And, in a completely unsentimental way, devout.

The chapel was warm and sweet with the smell of flowers and paraffin and a lingering wisp of incense— the nuns ended their day with Benediction and an hour's adoration of the Blessed Sacrament enshrined in a golden monstrance above the little tabernacle— and the shoes of the laity seemed to desecrate the spot-

less waxed floor. Never more than half a dozen parishioners came to those Masses, but in the tiny convent
chapel that was a crowd, and as the youngest Andrea
often had to settle for the doorway, half-in, half-out,
while the older women took the extra prie-dieux in the
back. How snowy white the linen was, how the glass
gleamed and the chalice glowed, and in the front, in-
distinguishable because of their veils, knelt the contingent of nine nuns assigned to the parish school.

That was the image of the religious life Andrea's
mother invoked. Did Andrea want to spend her life
like *that?* The truth was that her dreams of a vocation
had little to do with the parish nuns. They belonged to
the order of Saint Joseph of Carondolet, their habits
black, their headdress a starched pillbox over which
the veil fell to the shoulders. The starched expanse of a
massive unsplit Eton collar fell boardlike over the
bosom, and hanging on a cord that ran from the
neck under the wimple was a small black and gold
crucifix. The rustle of the heavy, full skirts, the clack
of the giant rosary that hung from the black cincture,
the somehow soundless black shoes with their Cuban
heels, a general air of ethereal otherworldliness must
have summed up Mrs. Bauer's notion of nuns. But
Andrea had encountered these seeming wraiths in the
classroom, and she had no illusions about their human
—all too human—qualities. They could be impatient,
they could be unkind, they could be, in one or two
cases, seemingly cruel to some hapless boy or girl. No,
when Andrea dreamed of life as a nun, she did not
imagine herself living out her days in one of those
rooms in the parish school or in the parish convent.

42

How could anything that familiar, that accessible, exercise a fascination for her?

She had discovered her vocation as the result of reading about the Little Flower, Sainte Thérèse de Lisieux, and Saint Rose of Lima. What she dreamed of was total abnegation, a complete rejection of the world as she hurled herself into an unknown future. The essence of her vocation was saying a definitive good-bye to everything familiar.

"The Little Flower was a Carmelite," Vera had said.

"I know."

"And Saint Rose was a Dominican."

"Yes, and Saint Clare was a Franciscan."

"You've never met a Franciscan."

"Would you approve if I wanted to become a Sister of Saint Joseph?"

"I know you never would."

"It's not my vocation."

"You mean you know what it's like. You just imagine the others will be different."

Andrea learned to regard the uneasiness she felt as a temptation, and she reacted accordingly by changing the subject. She had found a better confidant than Vera with whom to discuss such matters. He was Father Hurley, the new parish assistant in his first year as a priest.

Andrea calculated that Father Hurley was twenty-five years old. He was thin and pale, and his dark brown eyes seemed to regard her from spiritual depths she could scarcely imagine. Long years of study had finally brought him to the altar, and he was still living in the glow of the realization that he could say Mass, hear confessions, preach the Gospel, act as a bridge between God and man. He gave the phrase "first fervor" a permanent image for Andrea.

She mentioned her dream to him in the confessional, having whispered the few venial sins she had on her conscience, when Father Hurley told her to pray that she might learn God's will for herself.

"I want to be a nun, Father."

There was a pause during which his chair creaked on the other side of the grille. When he spoke again, he seemed to have moved closer to her. "I see."

"I have wanted to for a long time. I have written to several places and . . ."

Did she have a spiritual adviser? Had she talked with the nuns at the school, for instance? No. Another pause. Others were waiting to confess so this was not a good time, but he suggested she come by the rectory, where they could talk. Would she do that?

"Yes, Father."

"Just ask for me."

"Yes, Father."

"For your penance say five Our Fathers and five Hail Marys. And remember me in your prayers. Now say the Act of Contrition."

Talking with a priest put it on a higher level. This was in December of senior year. She had already had the date with Arthur when he held her tightly while something happened to him, and all obstacles seemed removed.

"But what do your parents think of this?"

"They don't like it. Particularly my mother."

"Doesn't she come to daily Mass quite often?"

"Yes, Father."

"It is difficult for parents to lose a child, as they think of it. Of course it is anything but that."

He sat behind the desk in one of the parish parlors, the buttons of his cassock rising to the starched white Roman collar, which seemed to hold his chin up. His dark hair was parted on the side and neatly combed. He was smoking a cigarette, and given the place and the topic, the smell of cigarette smoke took on an almost liturgical significance for Andrea. Years later, when, more out of defiance than desire, she took up smoking, the first tart smell of a freshly lit cigarette could bring back that parish parlor in almost total recall. The remembered scene could make her philosophical as she reflected that a future ex-nun and a future laicized priest had sat across a maple veneer desk talking about the will of God.

She was the young priest's first vocation, and he was extremely helpful, writing on her behalf to Green Bay, fending off the parish nuns who tried to turn her attention to their order, even talking with her parents, with her mother at the house and with her father at his dental offices. Maybe her father thought he could pick up a patient in the process.

If she felt any hesitation in telling her parents of her plans, it was out of concern for her father. As a late-arriving child and a daughter to boot, Andrea was very close to him. Still, she was not really surprised by his willingness to let her go. He could accept her leaving his world because his world had already left him.

Starting when she was a very little girl, they had

formed the habit of Saturday afternoon drives after his last appointment, and inevitably they would pay a visit to that part of Minneapolis where he had grown up and where his dental offices had been located for nearly twenty years. The area was now dominated by a great bouquet of cloverleafs which had been laid over an intersection that was called Seven Corners when her father was a boy. She became adept at imagining things where now there was only open space, a curving access road descending to the interstate that roared through the city, a grassy knoll where a single red-leafed maple, its thin trunk wrapped in burlap and twine, shivered in the constant movement of air created by traffic. The tree seemed never to grow. Perhaps it was not the same tree, but was replaced each year. Her father mordantly suggested they should use plastic greenery to adorn the place.

"Why not? They call all this concrete a cloverleaf."

There were set stations on this nostalgic *via crucis,* among them the coordinates that had once been occupied by the building in which Dr. Bauer began the practice of dentistry. That something so permanent and solid in appearance as that building could be annihilated had altered his sense of the seriousness of life. Nineteen years in a building that had been new when he first rented!

"Now I know what it must have been like in bombed-out cities."

He never spoke as if he were entirely serious about what he said, but Andrea was not deceived. That this neighborhood had been obliterated by urban renewal had cut him to the quick. The one remaining monument, apart from Holy Rosary Church, was a house in which her father had lived for three years as a boy. He had never thought of it as the real family home, but it was all that was left, and on several occasions they had crept slowly down the alley while he recalled long-ago episodes or parked in the street in front and surreptitiously studied the high frame house with flaking grayish paint. It had been subdivided and was now occupied by Indians, interracial couples, unsavory types.

"I wish they would knock down that house. And the church." He meant Holy Rosary.

"Then where would you go to Mass?"

Surprise gave way to a little smile, and after patting her hand he put the car in gear.

2.

Of course things changed a lot after she told her parents she intended to enter the convent. When Father Hurley first offered to come talk with them, Andrea hoped that would not be necessary. She had predicted to Vera that her mother would protest but nonetheless really understand her decision, while her father would do everything to dissuade her. She was wrong on both counts. Her father grew almost buoyant in the wake of the news, and one weekend, on their meandering drive, he asked why, when Andrea first told them of her plans, she had said some marriages end in divorce.

"Because they do."

Her father obviously wanted another answer. "How much has she told you, Andrea?"

"Who?"

"Your mother." He peered at her. "Was it Charlotte?"

"Told me what?"

After a time he shook his head, willing to believe she did not know what he was talking about but unwilling to tell her himself. That day he drew to the curb in front of Holy Rosary. It was a wide church that looked lower than it was, and its once rosy-colored stone had long since gone dark with soot.

"We were married there."

Andrea nodded, still confused. The church usually prompted her father to talk of when he had been an altar boy. This was where he went to Mass every Sunday morning, and he had always firmly refused to take her along. Andrea liked the thought of her father's devotion and his embarrassment about it.

"What did you think *Mother* told me?"

"Ask her." Without warning he put his arm around her and tugged her against him. They were not a demonstrative family, and his embrace was at once pleasant and uncomfortable. She was glad when he let her go. When she looked at him, she saw tears in his eyes. For five minutes she pressed her face against the passenger window, not wanting to see her father cry. Why on earth would a grown man weep? She decided he had been overcome by the thought of her eventual departure for the convent.

"I don't know what he had in mind," her mother

48

said, her lips a line not to be breached by the truth or any unsettling confidence.

"You must have some idea."

"Andrea, I quit trying to figure out your father years ago. The effort would have driven me mad."

In bits and pieces it came, from Charlotte, from her parents, until the point was reached when it was assumed she understood and there was no longer any need to conceal it.

"They've never been happy," Charlotte said. "You must have noticed that."

Happy? What did happiness have to do with them? Andrea had never regarded her parents' marriage as connected with anything as fragile and fugitive as moods.

"They never do anything together," her older sister said, continuing to comb young Larry's hair. She dipped a huge comb into a bottle of viscous green setting gel and arranged the thick blond hair on her son's head. How passive he was, how docile.

"They live together."

"It's not the same thing."

"Then what . . ."

Charlotte looked at her askance. What did she dare tell a girl still in school? Andrea had the dreadful thought that Charlotte was going to introduce the forbidden subject. Perhaps it was the presence of Larry that stopped her. "He never goes to church, Andrea. Does that tell you anything?"

"He goes to Holy Rosary!"

"What?"

"He gets up early and drives to Holy Rosary. He prefers it there. He was an altar boy when he was little."

Charlotte laughed.

"You kept us together," her mother finally told her. "He was going to leave, but when I became pregnant with you, of course he stayed."

It was difficult to know what to make of that. Had her mother half-consciously tempted her father into making love in order to keep him? Had her father deliberately created an obstacle to his own going?

"He was drunk, of course," her mother said, as if justifying herself.

Andrea would come to think of herself as the product of rape, conceived when her father, made amorous by liquor, had forced her mother and, as luck would have it, fertilized a waiting egg. She never did know quite what to make of this possibility, even when, convinced by Susan Brownmiller, she began to think of all sexual intercourse as a species of rape. Later, in the endless arguments over abortion, whenever someone said, as inevitably someone did, "But surely you can't be against abortion in the case of rape!" Andrea took it as an almost personal allusion. If her mother had been born a quarter of a century later, Andrea might have been suctioned from her womb and sent out with the trash.

But at the time of her mother's remark, it was the description of her father as drunk that shocked her.

"But Daddy doesn't drink."

"Daddy doesn't drink." Her mother repeated it as if it were a sentence in a foreign language.

"He doesn't!"

. . .

Charlotte said, "Honey, he's an alcoholic. He sneaks his drinks. That's why you've never seen him. What do you think happened to his practice?"

Her mother shook her head. "Charlotte shouldn't tell you these things. You don't have to know."

"Does Daddy drink?"

She nodded. "I'm surprised you never guessed. Well, maybe not. But there are bottles hidden around the house. And of course he drinks at the office."

The further awful revelations were tied to her father's drinking.

He had pleaded drunkenness when women patients began to complain. For years there had been unnecessary pats and pressures, nothing overt, nothing to cause alarm, until, misreading the message of a young matron, half of whose face was dead with novocaine, he had made the move that sent her screaming into the waiting room.

"I don't know why Mom was surprised," Charlotte said. "God knows, he got no affection at home. They're just waiting for you to grow up, and then they'll close up shop."

Did this explain her father's reaction to her vocation? The revelation that the home she had always thought so stable was held together by resentment, habit, and a sense of obligation to herself gave Andrea the dizzy feeling that nothing was what it seemed.

"Where does Daddy go on Sunday mornings?"

"To his office."

To drink. Now that Andrea looked for them, there

were signs all around the house of her father's alcohol-ism. Bottles in the basement, bottles in closets and drawers, a small bottle of brandy afloat in the tank of the toilet in the basement.

The move from his original offices, it seemed, had antedated the destruction of the building that had housed them. He had left because his practice had been destroyed by scandal. So he had moved into the low brick building whose parking lot melted into the giant one of the Stevenson Mall, sharing the building with an orthodontist, three dental aides, a chiropractor, an osteopathic surgeon, and a pharmacist. From the hous-ing development that had grown up quickly around the mall, he drew a sufficient number of patients to keep himself and his family afloat. Financially and in drink.

Her father died when she was a junior in college. She was allowed to come home for the funeral. He was buried from the church he had never attended, and his grandson, Larry, looking like a picture in cassock and surplice, was one of the altar boys. Her mother sat unweeping to Andrea's right, deriving strength from the presence of her daughter the nun. Charlotte and Willis shared the front pew with them. Willis seemed dis-tracted, and Charlotte cried shamelessly.

Dr. Bauer had been discovered on a Monday morn-ing by the cleaning crew in circumstances unbelievably bizarre. He had died of thrombosis, but his body was awash with alcohol and Librium and Seconal and other drugs. The office closet, when unlocked, looked like a liquor cabinet. Willis had been there when the door was opened and the policeman had involuntarily jumped back. Propped in a standing position inside the closet was an inflatable doll, life-size, absurdly equipped with breasts and female genitalia, an air-filled imaginary mate for the lonely drunken dentist. The office contained an abundance of pornography, video cassettes to be played on the large color television set, books, photographs, audio cassettes on which women groaned with desire and whispered nasty things into the listener's ear.

3.

Work was prayer. Scrubbing and cleaning and polishing, helping in the kitchen and the garden, helping in the laundry, ironing the refectory table cloth with the impression that beneath the board someone was manufacturing more and more linen and the job would never end. All that was prayer, and Andrea Bauer, postulant, half wished the ironing would go on forever. Prayer of the overt kind came only with difficulty. Had she ever really prayed before?

In chapel, kneeling all but motionless at her assigned place among the other postulants and novices, Andrea would expectantly close her eyes, but that only invited a stream of distracting images or brought on drowsiness. If she stared at the tabernacle, its lacy embroidered cover tied with a silken bow, all she could do was whisper formal prayers, the Our Father, the Hail Mary, or say her beads. But what she was supposed to be engaged in was mental prayer.

Sister Felicia, the novice mistress, was in her fifties,

apple-cheeked, with round steel-rimmed glasses, short, sweet. She spoke of prayer with almost sensuous delight. Andrea listened carefully to her instructions on the Ignatian method, the method the founder of the Jesuits had developed for his men. There were other methods, but Sister Felicia favored the Ignatian and recommended it to her charges.

What Andrea was to do was pick a theme, a virtue, a fault, and then choose an appropriate incident in Our Lord's life. The first step was to get the sense of place, to imagine as vividly as she could Jesus carrying his Cross, say, and then derive from it a lesson for her own life. The vividness of the image was meant to stir her heart to contrition and resolution. Her meditation was to end with a specific thought for the day, the implementation of the fruit of the meditation. At noon there was Particular Examen, when she was to look back over the morning and ask herself how she had done. Finally, at night she would examine her conscience and ask herself whether she had indeed during the day carried out the promise she had made to Jesus that morning. The day ended with the selection of the meditation theme for the following morning.

All this had been done for the postulants, a nun behind them breaking into the silence with a Gospel reading and, after another silence, some reflections on the story and lessons to be drawn from it. A suggested resolution for the day ended this collective meditation.

As a novice, however, Andrea, now called Sister Duns Scotus, was expected to meditate on her own, although she could consult Sister Felicia when necessary. And there was weekly confession, too, when she could discuss things with her confessor. Sister Felicia talked of prayer as if any minute not spent on one's knees in the chapel was wasted, but of course she quickly corrected that impression.

"Whatever you do throughout the day must be offered to God. Work, too, is prayer."

Andrea told her she found work prayer a lot easier than prayer prayer.

"Maybe you're trying too hard. When you kneel down, just put yourself in the presence of God. Remind yourself that you are his creature and that He created you from nothing and that you have come to worship and praise and thank and glorify him."

She left Sister Felicia resolved to master this essential technique of the religious, and she succeeded. Reading Teresa of Ávila, Francis de Sales, others, Andrea came to see her essential self as that inner silence into which she entered when she knelt before the tabernacle in the chapel. By the time she took her simple, temporary vows, she, like Sister Felicia, regarded the time spent in prayer as the precious, truly important part of her day.

And she saw better what it meant to say that work, too, is prayer. At first she had taken this to mean losing herself in the routine of her task and letting her mind take care of itself, but now, moving her iron back and forth across the board, washing, polishing, whatever, she was constantly referring what she did to God above, and as she glided through the corridors of the convent, she would stop before a plaster statue—Saint Joseph holding a lily, the Blessed Mother holding a pink, dimple-kneed baby Jesus, the Little Flower or Saint Francis—and let the sense of God's presence and that of his angels and saints take possession of her. She had made good, solid progress, and then her father died.

A few years' absence had separated her more completely from the world than she could have dreamed. Willis came for her in a car, and they drove to Minneapolis through the snowy Wisconsin countryside. An hour or so from the convent, it struck Andrea for the first time that her father was really dead. In the convent this had been an idea, abstract, pertaining to some other tense of time. The world, her parents, everything but her fellow religious, had become items of memory. Now, out in the palpable world, her father's death took on reality, and she could not stop herself from weeping.

This embarrassed Willis. It embarrassed Andrea, too, since she thought of it as weakness, a criticism of God's providence. She told herself that her father was now at home with God and that she must not weep as those who have no hope.

"He didn't feel a thing," Willis said.

Her brother-in-law had gained weight. He wore a camel's hair coat, the heater was on, and small beads of perspiration stood on his wrinkled brow.

"Are you sure?"

"He was sitting there alive, and then, whammo, the next minute he was dead."

"Without forewarning?"

Willis assured her there had been none. He had asked the doctor quite specifically.

"I didn't want Charlotte worrying about that."

Did he think she could take consolation from the fact that her father had been catapulted into eternity without even the opportunity to say an act of contrition? Where was he now, or, more specifically, where was his soul? That was the great and mysterious question, which Willis's clumsy attempt at reassurance only magnified.

Perhaps Willis considered Christian beliefs about the ultimate stakes of life only a literary matter, a theory of Dante or Milton, but Andrea lived in a world where these were vivid certainties. The meditations with which Saint Francis de Sales introduces one to a devout life had made hell and purgatory as real to her as heaven. The drama of life was that our passing deeds have an eternal significance; we freely decide our lasting condition by what we do in the brief time from cradle to grave. At death God puts his seal on the choice we have made. What had her father's choice been?

On the ride home her uneasiness had been generic, but when she learned the circumstances in which her father had died, Andrea almost despaired. If she did not, it was because of the prayers she had offered up daily for her parents, and for Charlotte and Willis and Larry, too. She had earned plenary indulgences for each of her parents; she had made the five First Saturdays for them and had commended them to Mary's motherly love. How delightful it was to read of souls snatched from Satan at the hour of death because of the intervention of the Blessed Virgin. A person of dissolute life had nonetheless worn the brown scapular of Our Lady of Mount Carmel, and at his death, true to her promise, Mary had claimed him for God. Andrea had sent her father a scapular, but when she learned how he had died, she feared it would invite derision of sacred things if she asked whether he had been wearing it when the attack took his life.

Charlotte and Willis had spared the ungrieving widow details of the scene of death. Willis had collected all the pornographic paraphernalia and brought it home. Andrea wished they had shown her as much consideration as they had her mother. Willis got out the dreadful stuff as if Andrea would take it in stride. A glimpse of the photographs was more than she could stand, and she drew back, appalled.

"Dear God," she whispered.

"It's sad," Charlotte agreed, riffling through a magazine while Andrea kept her eyes averted. "Better get rid of this, Will. I wouldn't want Larry to see it."

"Should I put on one of the video cassettes?"

Willis seemed anything but disinterested in his late father-in-law's secret cache of pornography. The television screen filled with unbelievable acts, and Andrea fled the room. Charlotte came after her, and, embraced by her older sister, Andrea wept despairingly.

"He's well out of it, Andrea. Life was not really very kind to him. He drank himself to death, but there are worse things."

"But those awful pictures."

"I don't blame him."

It might have been an admonition not to judge, but that is not how Charlotte meant it.

"Whatever works, Andrea. Mother froze him out; he had to turn to something. And the scandal with that patient had frightened him. Dirty pictures are safe."

It was not a conversation Andrea wanted to continue.

How could she accept her sister's viewpoint? On the other hand, to remind Charlotte of the true significance of their father's behavior would have been even more depressing. Eventually she spent forty-five minutes with Father Hurley, and that was a blessing.

"I worry about him, Father."

She sat where she had sat as a high school girl, in the some rectory parlor, but now she wore the habit of a nun. Across the desk Father Hurley wore a dark cardigan, and his shirt, a regular man's shirt, was open at the neck. The few years had matured him; he possessed the authority of experience now. But Andrea missed the brand new priest whose countenance had seemed to shine with an otherworldly glow.

"I'll continue to remember him in my Mass."

"Thank you, Father."

"You've changed." He smiled as he carefully tapped ashes from his cigarette.

"I hope so."

"You're content?"

She nodded. "Very. I can hardly wait to get back."

"What are you doing in terms of renewal there?"

There was to be a meeting the coming summer. On the agenda were the governance of the order, methods of election and representation, procedures to be taken if one was unjustly treated, the habit. Father Hurley bobbed his head with each item.

"Good. Will the novices have any say in all this?"

"I myself will be taking part."

"You will! Tell me about it." He put out his cigarette and leaned toward her, elbows on the desk, unmistakably excited.

"I was elected."

"Congratulations!"

His reaction surprised her. When she was told of her election, Andrea had been neither pleased nor displeased. If she was asked to attend the meeting, she would attend the meeting. She did not particularly look forward to it. She certainly had not regarded it as a triumph to be asked.

"Who elected you?"

"Mother Superior."

"She elected you?"

"That's right."

"What kind of election is that? I thought you meant you had been chosen by the other novices to represent them."

Andrea did not like his criticism of Mother Superior and found it an odd idea that novices should pick someone as their representative. Being a novice was not a permanent condition. One aspired to be a full member of the order. In the meanwhile, and afterward, too, one did as one's superior bade one do.

Father Hurley seemed to think she was joking when she said this.

"Don't you know it," he whispered, glancing toward the hallway. "Guess who's mad as blazes because my name is on the ballot for the priests' senate?"

This was a post-conciliar innovation, and it was obvious that Father Hurley was enthusiastic about it and quite openly critical of the way the pastor, Monsignor Quinlan, was dragging his feet, resisting the clear directives of the council Fathers.

"He keeps quoting canon law when I bring it up. Canon law! Can you imagine? The fact that the code is being rewritten doesn't faze him. 'It continues to be the law of the Church until it is changed.' "

His imitation of the pastor was so good that Andrea had to laugh. That melted her resistance and soon they were chattering away about the future envisaged by the council.

"You're the future," he assured her. "The old ones are the past. There are bound to be clashes, but we will win. A lot of old priests would like to ignore the council, turn back the clock, keep the clerical club secure. Well, those days are gone forever, and I for one am glad."

Father Hurley could not wait until there was more lay participation in the administering of the parish, and in liturgical functions, too. "And I mean women as well as men."

How could she not respond favorably to that? He surprised her by going on and seeming to suggest, if she understood him—he spoke very elliptically—that the day would come when women would be ordained priests! It was her first introduction to a topic that would become central in her life.

"How is your mother holding up?"

Her mother was doing fine. It was Andrea who needed help, though what anyone could do to expunge from her mind hell and eternal punishment and the awful circumstances in which her father had died, she did not know.

"Mother is doing fine."

61

Father Hurley shook his head. "People never cease to amaze me."

"How do you mean?"

"Their ability to absorb pain and tragedy and go on." He lit another cigarette. "I see it every day."

4.

Vera had come to the wake, but she kept as close to her parents as Andrea did to her mother. By the time they came through the line, Andrea knew that either people had prepared a brief remark or they genuinely did not know what to say. "I'm so sorry. Such a sad thing. He was such a good person." In everyone's manner seemed to be the alarming realization that death would come inevitably for them, that the body in the coffin would one day be oneself. But there were some who just stopped and took her hand and stared silently with tear-filled eyes. Vera fell somewhere between the two types. "Oh, Andrea," she said, her voice breaking.

But the tears in Vera's case might have been as much for the sight of her old friend in religious garb as for her loss. It was Andrea's first appearance in her habit in these old haunts.

"I hope we can talk."

"How long are you home?"

They got together two days after the funeral, meeting, at Andrea's insistence, downtown. It was a bit of an adventure driving in the habit, another first, and a further adventure going to a restaurant with Vera.

"I wasn't sure you could," Vera said as they settled at a table in Dayton's Tearoom.

Andrea smiled. She wasn't sure herself. Strictly speaking, she should not be traveling without a fellow religious, but this rule had been waived as unnecessary since Willis was coming for her and she would be staying with her mother. No one had given any thought to meeting old friends for lunches downtown. It was a situation in which one had to use common sense, and Andrea used hers in favor of a good talk with her old friend.

"You look . . . striking."

Well, she could hardly expect Vera to ignore what she was wearing. Andrea felt the beginning of an uncharacteristic blush. The truth was, she had something of the feeling of dressing up, of being an impostor. It would have been impossible to ignore the reactions of the other diners as they were led to their table. To say that Andrea was the only nun in the tearoom was not merely a contingent fact, as if others might drop in later. Nuns did not eat in public places.

"I thought I was used to it, but it is different being out in the world dressed like this."

"Can't you wear civvies at home?"

She told Vera that this was her normal dress, that it represented far more than clothing. When she was given the habit, it had been a very solemn occasion, a ceremony that had begun with Andrea in a wedding dress and ended with her in this very same habit. She sensed that she was going on at too great a length, but she could not stop. It seemed important that Vera understand. And maybe she was remembering what she had done that morning.

At home, in her own room, she had tried on an old pair of jeans and a sweater. Standing before the mirror she had stared at herself for ten minutes. It was as if her years in the convent had never been. Why on earth had her mother kept all these clothes? The drawers of the dresser were full; in the closet hung a row of dresses, ghostly memories of her earlier self.

But it was the earlier self that was more real now, at home, with Vera. Looking at herself in the mirror, Andrea had had the feeling she was doing something vaguely illicit, wearing these old clothes. But she had exchanged the jeans for a dress and had spent hours slipping into and out of her old wardrobe, each time confronting a different yet very familiar self in the mirror. Her hair was cut quite short in order to fit under her headdress, but it had retained its shape. Parted in the middle, very full, a red so dark it was like mahogany. Her face looked longer because of the shortness of her hair, but then it looked almost oval in her habit. Large eyes that took in more than they let out, her nose a little too thin but with an interesting diamond-shaped bone on the bridge. Round chin and a mouth whose lips were generous. They would one day be called sensuous. In the privacy of her own room, it seemed permitted to notice that her breasts were, if anything, fuller and more shapely than before. It was that realization that had prompted her to slip back into her habit, hang up all those clothes, and go confusedly downstairs.

64

"At least it looks comfortable," Vera said in Dayton's Tearoom.

"Is that the best you can say?"

"I don't think it will become the fashion, if that's what you mean."

"Actually we may change it. There is a meeting scheduled for next summer, when it will be discussed, along with more important things."

"Tell me about your life."

She did, of course, not quite consciously assuming that her own life was ever so much more narratable than Vera's. Vera was at St. Catherine's, but that just meant more Sisters of Saint Joseph of Carondolet. Talking of her own life, Andrea found it even more interesting than it was, and of course she wanted to convey to her old friend how happy she was as a nun. This was the life she had wanted, and, by the grace of God, she had it. On her side Vera seemed endlessly interested in everything Andrea had to say.

"You must come visit, Vera. We have guest rooms; you would be very welcome. I'll never forgive you for not coming to my profession."

Not quite true. Andrea would not even have cared if her parents had decided against the long drive to Green Bay when their youngest daughter was invested in the habit. Knowing what she then knew of them, Andrea preferred praying for her parents from a distance to trying to behave with them as if everything were as she had for so long thought it was between them. But they came, and Charlotte and Willis came, too, and there was a festive reception afterward. Andrea

65

had felt stared at, much as she now did in Dayton's Tearoom.

"But tell me about you. Is there a boy?"

Vera smiled. "No one special."

"What is your major?"

"Don't laugh. Philosophy."

"Laugh? Don't be silly. It's mine, too, more or less. I have to take enough credits for a major whether I want to or not, but I want to. I love it. What classes have you taken?"

Andrea told Vera of her own classes, of epistemology, metaphysics, philosophy of man, general and special ethics; she talked about the Euclidean cleanness of the argumentation that had attracted and held her. She was shocked when Vera said her professor had expressed doubt that any of the proofs of God's existence were sound.

"He cannot mean Duns Scotus's. I would defend his proof to the death."

"I don't know it."

Vera had been given only the five ways of Saint Thomas. The friar who had taught Andrea metaphysics had been insistent on the respect they all owed Saint Thomas Aquinas. It should never be forgotten that the Church had singled Thomas out from among the Schoolmen. With that piously out of the way, they had settled down to study Scotus. They were assigned parallel readings in Thomas, of course, but Scotus seemed all the more satisfying after the thinness of Aquinas. Vera on the other hand had never even heard of the *De primo principio*. It was Andrea's first acquaintance with the hegemony of Thomism, and the resentment she felt there in Dayton's Tearoom was destined to grow and expand and finally to encompass a good deal more than a style of philosophy and theology.

The most surprising news of the luncheon was Vera's almost casual remark that she intended to go on to law school after graduation.

"Good heavens."

"Don't you approve?"

Andrea just laughed, but she really didn't approve. Did she disapprove? It seemed better to describe her reaction as uncertain, and that was because she had never really thought of Vera as a lawyer. She had no available image of a woman lawyer. The alternative to the life she led had been the life led by her own mother and Vera's. A woman's vocation—per se, as Scotus would have said—is to be a wife and mother. Not that Andrea needed the help of Scotus to think so. It had been her own unquestioned if unstated conviction all her life. Becoming a nun had meant turning away from motherhood and a family, and one developed an apologia for it on that basis. She had the funny idea that Vera was thinking of becoming a sort of nun without entering the convent.

"Tell me about all those boys."

"You probably already know most of them."

"Don't tell me one of them is Arthur!"

"No, not Arthur!"

They both remembered the same episode, apparently, and an embarrassed silence fell.

PART THREE

Lovers of a Sort

I.

Vera shopped on the Via Sistina, then made her way down the outdoor bazaar that had flowered on the Spanish Steps. Dissolute youths from a dozen nations, their twisted wire junk jewelry spread out on cloth before them, looked up at her with indolent brazenness. The girls with them, having bade adieu to middle-class morality, seemed to be devising one of their own, petulant expressions warning that the man they had slept with was theirs alone. Were they learning that the easy giving of their unbathed bodies to these narcissistic males decreased their bargaining value? Perhaps kicking off the traces, thumbing one's nose at the old virtues, presented problems of its own. Vera wondered briefly how Edward was enjoying his new life, then drove the thought away.

She stopped to listen to a man playing a ceramic ocarina so small it was all but concealed by his hands. She was amazed at the music he got from it. Displayed at his sneakered feet were models of various sizes, their leather throngs suggesting they were to be worn around the neck. She bought two of the medium-size ones, eliciting a smile featuring a gold tooth that might have been the secret of his virtuosity. Gifts? Perhaps. One of her postponed dreams had been to learn to play something

—the guitar, the piano. The ocarina might very well be her musical destiny.

Flowers, music, junk jewelry—the Spanish Steps seemed a Gypsy place, but these, she had been told, were the children of the bourgeoisie, and that seemed plausible. The pairings often involved an extremely young girl and a man in his late twenties or early thirties. Vera was almost disappointed by the apparent joylessness of it all.

At the bottom of the steps was the house in which Keats had died, become a kind of private museum into which Vera did not go. Perhaps another time. Keats. She looked up the steps that flanked his shrine at the young girls and men through whom she had just threaded her way. Couples. Male and female. Forever he pursues and she pursued. Figures on a vase seemed a better way to prolong and make permanent the momentary pleasure of sex. How could you make a career of somethng so fleeting unless you froze it on a vase or preserved it in fidelity and love?

She was becoming a lady preacher. She picked up the *Herald Tribune* and the *Rome Daily American* and went on to the Caffè Greco, where, in one of the plush back rooms, she ordered tea from a fat waiter in a swallowtail coat, who studied himself in the mirror behind her.

"Milk or lemon?" he asked in British tones. Apparently he disapproved of her attempt to speak Italian.

"Limone."

One eyebrow appeared in comment above his thick glasses, and he tipped his head ever so slightly.

"Subito, signora."

A happy life is the sum of small victories. Vera opened her paper with the sense of having established who was the waiter and who the patron. Forever he pursues and she presides.

Her stay in Rome was made up of sightseeing, shopping, and sitting in restaurants and cafés, then falling exhausted into her bed in the Columbus Hotel. All that and trying not to worry about Katy. Twice she had returned home to find a note indicating her niece had stopped by, but whenever she had tried to reach her, the phone had been answered by some chuckleheaded girl who asked Vera to wait. Katy never came to the phone, and having listened to nothingness for twenty minutes or so, Vera had put the almost weightless dove gray phone back into its cradle with an inadequate bang. This morning she had taken a cab to Katy's address and left a note of her own. "Meet me at the Pantheon at seven tonight."

Seven so she could take her niece to dinner, the Pantheon because she needed a landmark, tonight because Vera did not know how much longer she intended to stay in Rome. Athens, Paris, London? It made her dizzy to think that, simply by deciding, she could fly off to any of those. Or to all of them.

Her tea came, and while she fussed with it, she thought of that long-ago luncheon in Dayton's Tearoom when Andrea, home for her father's funeral, was so absurdly vain about her religious habit. Did she really imagine that she was admired? Or envied? What Vera had felt was embarrassment—human respect, as Andrea would have called it. Out to lunch with a nun. Ye gods.

Andrea had floated in ahead of her like a model. "Next, Sister Duns Scotus wearing a traditional number, full black skirt, white ropy cincture, with veil." A pirouette would not have surprised Vera. Leaving the world seemed to be a species of self-absorption. Her veil lined with starched linen sat like an open book on her head, the headdress reminiscent of the way Andrea had usually worn her hair, parted in the middle, framing her face.

The mention of Arthur was something from which they talked themselves away for the rest of the luncheon. Vera was almost shocked that Andrea, in her condition of professional virginity, still recalled the episode. But then why had she remembered it herself? She was as much a virgin as Andrea, a condition she thought of not as an accomplishment, but certainly as temporary. Despite that, she had gone on about her legal ambitions in a way that did not accurately reflect her mind. She would have much preferred to live her life at someone's side, to encourage and promote her husband's ambitions and in return to be cherished and protected by him. And there was the vague thought of children, vague not because she doubted she wanted them, but because being a mother seemed as unimaginable as going to heaven. Holding Dolores's latest baby could make law school seem a silly diversion. Out of the cradle, endlessly rocking . . .

If the allusion to Arthur had come as a bit of a shock, Vera was still more surprised when she asked Andrea what she liked best about being a nun.

"Praying."

She was as serious as could be. Vera had not known what to say, so she repeated the answer.

"I suppose that sounds odd—it would have sounded odd to me a few years ago—but think of it, Vera. God exists. He is everywhere. He is with us now. Prayer is simply acknowledging that."

The thought of God's hanging around Dayton's Tearoom told Vera how little she and her friend still had in common. Thank God Andrea had not gone on about it. Yet it was that remark that had stayed with her through the years, to recur with particular urgency since her divorce, though the Andrea who had spoken of prayer across the luncheon table in Minneapolis no longer existed, having been superseded by a whole series of later versions, culminating in the one who had slipped into bed with Edward.

In that side chapel in St. Peter's, itself the size of a church, where the Blessed Sacrament was exposed each morning at the end of the nine o'clock Mass, Vera had sat on, staring at the brilliant monstrance, at its center the translucent disk that was Jesus in the form of bread. But she was distracted by the two nuns who entered the chapel and took their stations in front of the altar, blue veils covering not only their heads but their bodies, so that Vera never saw their faces. After they knelt, they remained motionless for fifteen minutes, then stood in unison and sat bolt upright on the chairs behind their prie-dieux. They alternated kneeling and sitting every quarter hour. Watching them, Vera was reminded again of Andrea's striking definition of prayer: simply the acknowledgment of God's presence.

What in God's name would it be like if she concentrated on the things in which, ostensibly, she believed, the tenets of the faith she had never rejected even during the years when her practice of it had been all but nil? "God made me to know him, to love him and to serve him in this world and to be happy with him forever in the next." But there was so much more than that. God had become a man in a semiarid land and had worked wonders for a band of illiterate followers who were the predecessors of bishops and priests and whose word she had that Jesus was risen from the dead as a sign of our own future destiny.

Beneath the main altar of this basilica lay the remains of St. Peter himself. Like Paul he had come to Rome, and like Paul he had been put to death here. Her faith involved connection with these events, unmemorable at the time, a passing on of power, power to forgive sins and to turn the bread and wine into Jesus on the altar.

Letting these beliefs slide past her mind, savoring their incredibility, Vera gave her assent to them all. Improbable? Of course they were. That there is a God who is everywhere is already improbable enough. That there is anything whatever is the most improbable thing of all.

Such thoughts made it sound like arguing. Vera had no desire to argue with these truths. She embraced them; she did not understand them, she believed them. One of the least expected results of Edward's leaving her was the realization that she had something a good deal more solid than his fragile promise on which to lean.

2.

"You seem to have seen a lot of churches," Katy said that night. They were sitting, the three of them, Katy and Kenneth the seminarian and Vera, in the Trattoria Madellena, which was about a block from the Pantheon, their waiter a portly man with a fiercely be-whiskered face and eyes that squinted in a smile.

"Even the Pantheon is a church."

"Sure, a pagan one."

"No," said Ken. "It is a Christian church."

Vera felt she detected a faintly proprietary tone in his voice.

She said, "And one where you can get a plenary in-dulgence."

"What?" Katy's nose wrinkled cutely.

"Ken will have to explain that to you."

"It's a long story," he said dubiously. He seemed more amused than startled by her remark.

Vera had showed up in the square in front of the Pantheon twenty minutes before the appointed time and had taken an outdoor table, paying for it by ordering an overpriced Coke. The sun still slanted into the piazza, which was as busy as any place Vera had been in Rome. Young people like those she had seen on the Spanish Steps lounged on an obelisk monument in the center of the square. The great bronze doors of the Pantheon were closed now. Ten times the height of a man, shaded by the porch of the building that had been erected before the Christian era, they had opened to pagans when Peter and Paul were in this city but had long since been given over to the strange worship those men had come to preach. Now, in the post-Christian era, there was a brisk business in soft drugs going on around Vera. The smell of strange smoke from the next table had caught her attention, and then it became obvious that many of those in the square were high.

When she saw Katy, her impulse was to get up and go quickly to her niece, but the realization that the young man beside Katy was with her kept Vera in her chair. It was an advantage, being able to see Katy before she herself was recognized and to study the boy she had no doubt was the Ken of whom she had heard. How Katy felt about him was all too obvious, but the boy's manner was difficult for Vera to read. He seemed at ease with Katy; there was nothing furtive about him. But then, if Katy was right, he was breaking no rules by going about with her. Why did he do it? Simply because he enjoyed her company? That it was all an experiment, a thought too reminiscent of Andrea, angered Vera. She was damned if she wanted her niece used as a lab animal to help some self-centered boy determine whether or not he wanted to live a celibate life. She got up from her table and moved swiftly toward her niece.

It was not until he spoke, with the faintest trace of sarcasm in his tone, of the plenary indulgence to be had visiting certain designated churches in Rome that Vera had a natural opening to inquire into Ken's status.

"Katy says you're in the North American College."

"This is my second year."

"Do you like it?"

He thought about it. "It's all right."

"You don't sound very enthusiastic."

"After you've been here awhile, it loses some of its enchantment."

"Where are you from?"

"You've never heard of it."

"Try me."

"Mankato. It's a town in—"

"Minnesota."

"How did you know that?"

"Because I'm a native of Minneapolis. I grew up there. If I hadn't gone to law school at Loyola, I might never have moved to Chicago. I might never have visited it. Except to see Katy's mother, of course."

He hunched over the table and grinned at her. He did have a certain boyish charm, with the emphasis on "boyish." When did boys turn into men? Some never did, and she wondered if Ken, like her Edward, was one of them. He seemed genuinely surprised that anyone besides him could be from Minnesota.

"Aren't there any other students for the priesthood from Minnesota?" There, she had gotten it onto the table.

"Not studying for my diocese."

"When will you be ordained?"

Beneath the table Vera felt Katy's kick.

"I have two years after this one."

"Will you be ordained here in Rome?"

"That's up to the bishop." He had hesitated before speaking, as if sensing the topic was an odd one in this company. "I hope you don't think there's anything wrong with my being here with you."

"Wrong?" Vera thought her tone was appropriately incredulous, but she got another kick for her pains. "My best girl friend became a nun."

Katy sat back at this non sequitur, her mouth open in disbelief, but Ken seemed to find some logical link. Vera herself did not know what it was until Ken asked what order her friend belonged to.

"She's no longer a nun. She left."

"Oh. What is she doing now?"

How tempting it was to answer that with a blithe "Oh, she's living with my ex-husband, without benefit of clergy, but what the hell, we're all adults now, aren't we?" Instead she told a simpler truth, which to her was just as preposterous.

"She's a counselor."

Ken nodded. Of course. Screwing up one's own life seemed a prerequisite for advising others on how to screw up theirs. Edward had sought Andrea as a counselor when his secret smoking had filled him with such self-loathing that he needed a sympathetic ear into which to pour resentment of his domineering wife.

"I'm told she's quite good."

"Nuns often have a special gift for pastoral work, in hospitals, on parish teams. They're only a step or two from the priesthood now."

"My friend dreamed of being ordained."

Ken's face clouded. There was already something fistlike about his face in repose, but now it seemed to fold further in upon itself. "It is ridiculous to say that women don't deserve ordination."

"Or that men do?"

"You mean just because they're men?"

Vera had moved her foot out of range of Katy's kick. "Something like that."

3.

There is a pathological process, Vera decided, whereby people move in well-defined stages from true to false religion. Not that she was interested in this as an abstract problem. She had first sensed it in reflecting on the trajectory Andrea had taken, but this boy reminded her so powerfully of the Andrea of graduate school that it was uncanny. He was at the stage where the talk was more or less unchanged, but the meanings differed. This was the stage at which Andrea had patiently explained to her that the reason for dropping the habit was so she and her fellow nuns—why did "fellow nuns" sound so funny?—could more effectively do their job.

"It's hard to pray in the habit?"

Andrea's smile was sweet enough to kill. "We did not enter the convent to escape the world."

The obverse of which was that she was not coming back into the world in order to leave the convent. But nonetheless there she was, back in the world, a knockout in a polka-dot dress, a navy blue silk scarf arranged artlessly around her throat, her thick hair grown almost shoulder length, falling in two great parentheses from its central part to enclose a face from which two very

large, very sincere green eyes looked into Vera's. Which
dropped to the ever-so-slightly freckled hand Andrea
had put upon her sweatered arm. Vera had the over-
powering feeling that the world, and she in particular
as a modest inhabitant of it, was going to know that
Andrea was back.

"Back" was graduate school at Marquette University
in Milwaukee to pursue an M.A. in theology, with an
eventual eye to teaching at her order's college in Green
Bay. The order would foot the bill; Andrea, in civvies,
would share an apartment with two other nuns; and
there was the prospect that in her second semester she
might be taken on by the campus ministry in some
capacity or other. Andrea had come to Chicago to see
Vera, who was about to start her second year of law
school at Loyola.

"Is it hard?" Andrea asked.

"Only the first year, and that's behind me." She had
wondered if they would ever get around to what she
was doing. Andrea was the magnetic north of all con-
versational navigation, and unless sighted from star-
board, Vera did not exist.

"What was the hardest?"

"Torts."

"What else?"

"Retorts." Andrea did not even smile, but then she
was not really listening. Vera resisted complaining about
contract law. "Tell me what you will be studying?"

If Andrea was not really interested in the law cur-
riculum, she could not hear enough of how Vera lived,
her friends, her future. It might have been flattering if

Andrea had not been trying on these descriptions as possible roles.

Vera had not realized all this then, of course. Retrospective omniscience came, by definition, later. If she felt anything at the time, it was that Andrea's move from convent life to that apartment in Milwaukee and her prospective studies in theology were intrinsically more interesting than her own humdrum existence as a law student in Chicago, a city through which she passed as one blind, her day defined by classes and books.

"No dates?"

"I go out with other students, sure."

"Men."

"Do you know how many women there are in law school?"

"How would I know? Is there someone special?"

It seemed an obligation to make much of Fred Durkin, an awkward genius six and a half feet tall who had bought her coffee a lot and seemed to like being with her in the student lounge. He was eloquent on anything legal, otherwise tongue-tied, and if this was romance, Vera was an alien from another planet.

"Six and a half feet tall!"

Andrea's glee seemed an oblique comment on Vera's height.

"And that's lying down." My God, it had just slipped out, an ill-considered, poor attempt at a joke. Andrea blinked twice, the second time keeping her eyes closed as she slowly turned her head and tilted her chin. Portrait of a virgin. What in heaven's name would she think Vera was? On the other hand, the role of fallen

83

woman, however unearned, had its attractions. You would have thought that being a second-year law student was more than enough to counter whatever superiority she imagined Andrea to have, but it wasn't. So she had not denied the implication of Andrea's turning away.

"You'd like him. Everyone does."

Which was true enough. If you had difficulty understanding anything, Fred was more than willing to help. The last Vera had heard of him, he was on the short list for appointment to the appellate court.

"I gather it's serious."

"Between us? Heavens no."

In the context, that added fickleness to promiscuity and provided more than enough excuse to get back to the subject of Andrea, the New Nun, and what the fathers of Vatican II wanted in terms of renewal for the Church. Dull? Andrea sounded like Theodore White describing a political campaign.

"Do you remember Bill Hurley?"

Vera frowned in confusion.

"Quinlan's assistant. The young priest."

"Father Hurley?" Vera had never known the assistant pastor's first name.

"Quinlan asked to have him moved, you know. The whole thing is there in a nutshell. You have the old guard in the form of Quinlan—Monsignor Quinlan." As who should say, So and So, esquire. "And you have the new generation in Bill Hurley. Quinlan can't deny that the council occurred, though he would probably like to, so what he has to do is pretend that all it did was underwrite the way it has always been. Pastors running a tight ship, assistants and parishioners doing what they are told. Any suggestion that this is not what the conciliar documents say infuriates him.''

It certainly sounded dramatic enough. Good guys, bad guys. The forces of reaction against the progressives. Champions of the people against a band of autocrats.

That essential conversation continued over the years, but Andrea changed. She was no longer wearing the polka-dot dress, but a fitted tweed suit that brought out the red in her hair. And then the blue-gray silk blouse, her waist cinched with a leather belt and a great, flowing purple skirt that fell below the knee. Andrea was wearing makeup, too, a little lipstick, eye shadow, the slightest touching up of the lashes. There must be no barriers between nuns and the people. But who would take her for a nun anymore? She had completed her master's at Marquette and come on to the University of Chicago, to the divinity school.

"It was a battle, let me tell you."

"How so?"

There were good nuns and bad nuns, too, it emerged, and some elderly sisters had opposed Andrea's pursuit of a doctorate, particularly at a godless secular school.

"It is a waste of time trying to explain the Theology Union to them."

"Then explain it to me."

Vera never got it right, perhaps, but it seemed that graduate studies in theology at the University of Chicago were either nondenominational or multidenominational, depending on how you wanted to put it.

"Call it ecumenical," Andrea said. "Ecumenical" was one of those words that when spoken by Andrea seemed freighted with significance. Vera said it was odd the way Catholics couldn't speak English since the vernacular had been introduced, but Andrea was singularly lacking in a sense of humor about such matters.

"Having Mass in English is one of the best things to come out of the council."

Vera let it go. After passing the bar she had been taken on for peanuts at Patterson, Patterson, Flood and Barrett. She worked like a Trojan and, on Sundays, slept late. Mass was no longer the regular thing it had been. Andrea, however, was not shocked.

"It should not be legalistic. That is the old Church. Doing things by the numbers, by rote, without engaging the mind and heart."

Vera had met Edward by then, and, in an odd way, when their relationship became serious, when marriage loomed, the fact that they were both Catholic seemed as important as anything else about them. Her sister, Dolores, insisted that Vera must be married in her parish church.

4.

Edward.

Edward the absurd. But that came later, much later. At first he was simply Edward, and she loved him from the start, not understanding why, not really caring. The major delight of the feeling was that it was a feeling, not an argument, a wholly different use of her mind from that which occupied her all day at Patterson, Pat-

terson, Flood and Barrett. Passing through the reception
room that fateful day, she was attracted by the awkward
way he attempted to look at ease. She paused to ruffle
the magazines and overheard his inquiry. He had come
in to start a Keogh plan, and though this was not at all
Vera's specialty, indeed was the kind of thing for which
PPF&B would usually recommend a bank, she indicated
from her position behind the visitor that she was available, jabbing an index finger at her head and making
eloquent faces at Ruth, the receptionist.

"Days she doesn't come in are described as ruthless, of
course."

Was it his laughter that won her? It was a change,
having her wit appreciated. On the premises it drew
mainly frowns, particularly from Ruth, who in any case
regarded it as demeaning that she should be at the beck
and call of another female.

"It's good of you to see me right away like this. If
someone came to my office without an appointment . . ."

"What line of business are you in, Mr. . . . ?"

"Doctor. Dr. Thorne. I'm a dentist."

Vera closed her mouth in self-defense, while she tried
to think of a way she could find out exactly how to set
up a retirement plan for self-employed individuals without revealing to Dr. Thorne that she knew as little about
it as he did.

He was looking around her office, clearly impressed,
but that was the main point of offices at Patterson, Patterson, Flood and Barrett: red leather, brass, what might
be mahogany or teak, wall-to-wall maroon carpet with a
few small orientals to relieve the modernity.

"I spend most of my day standing up," he said.

"Doing open-mouth surgery?"

His laugh began with an initial bark, head thrown back, and then proceeded to a dying series of gasping sounds, ending with a few chuckles while he looked right at her. His eyes squinted nicely. He was attractive in an unhandsome way. Manly. Very large hands, which had to be less than a blessing in his profession. A frieze of fuzz on the backs of them. Did they tickle the patient's upper lip as he probed?

They ended up in the library, making a little research project of it. She would instruct him in the nature of the Keogh plan while learning all about it herself. Dudley, who normally did these things, if they were done at all, looked in, probably informed by Ruth, shrugged, and went away. No resentment, apparently. Good. Anyway, it served him right. She had given Dudley every encouragement, only to have his behavior justify that first syllable of his name.

"Don't you have appointments today?"

"On Wednesday?"

"The dental Sabbath?"

Ho, ho, they got along just fine. They drew up his plan, and Dudley checked it over and it flew, and by the time they had decided to have dinner together, she knew his annual income, his address, his next of kin—Mom and Dad—and that she could elicit a laugh from him even with the lowest of puns. Liking him was largely a matter of knowing he liked her, and what was wrong with that?

He talked her out of going home to change; she looked just fine the way she was. So did he. Blazer, gray flannels, striped shirt, knit tie, and loafers. She had seen

him in a million magazine ads, but somehow that was
reassuring. He represented solidity. A professional man.
Already established. Twenty-nine years old. He had put
in four years in the army after graduating from dental
school.

"Colgate?"

By this time he was punching her arm before chuck-
ling. Northwestern. Right here in Chicago. The army
had paid his undergraduate expenses and picked up
dental school as well. After four years of slavery— "in-
dentured servitude?" Punch, chuckle—he was settled
down, raking in money, anxious to get some of it out of
the immediate grasp of Uncle Sam. Hence what they
were calling, between them, his Keyhole plan.

"Remember the Knothole Gang?"

He didn't. But then he had grown up in Evansville,
Indiana, not Minneapolis. How could he have known
of Halsey Hall, WCCO, and Killer Killibrew? As if in
compensation he was a hockey fan, so she told him of
winters in Minneapolis, hockey in the streets, on the
frozen lakes, on Minnehaha Creek above the falls. She
told him of the facsimile of Longfellow's house that
stood on the banks of the creek there.

"By the shore of Gitche Gumee."

She felt comfortable with him. Maybe because she
had no parents to explain to him. Her mother had con-
tracted cancer but died of a heart attack incurred when
she was hurrying to her chemotherapy session. By then
Alzheimer's disease had reduced her father to a vegetable condition. His death a few years later seemed
somehow posthumous.

What had she and Edward eaten that first night? It

could have been cornflakes. A week after she met him, she took him to meet Dolores.

"Her husband was assigned here temporarily twelve years ago."

"What does he do?"

"His explanation would be more intelligible than mine."

The men got along; Howard even turned down the sound of the television as they talked. Edward listened as to an authority; Howard nodded attentively when the young dentist spoke. Dolores gave Vera a look. Destiny was in the air.

"What's his sign?"

"He's a Catholic, Dolores."

But Dolores insisted on knowing the date of Edward's birth.

"Pisces," she said thoughtfully.

"What am I?"

"Virgo, I hope."

Her sister spoke of porches and conjunctions and other nonsense. There was a bit of the Gypsy about Dolores. The children rushed through from time to time, passing from the playroom in the basement to the bedrooms above. Dolores asked Edward to check her son's retainer.

"Personally, I think it's nothing but a rip-off. How can that straighten teeth?"

Edward was nice about it, smiled, took a perfunctory peek into little Jimmy's mouth. Howard, sensitive about his dentures, did not like the conversation to linger too long on teeth.

They went to Blackhawks games and lost their minds

for three periods, then filed out shamefacedly with the other fans. *Post agonem triste.* It was like a vacation from reason. It was like being in love. After they had known one another a month, they went to talk with Dolores's pastor.

The rectory was an efficient as a dental office—Edward's comparison. Marriage? Right. Do them all the time. They were given a mimeographed sheet enumerating the papers they would need. It was an archdiocesan requirement that they attend at least a Cana weekend. Refusal would have been a Cana mutiny. Bad, but the pastor was Italian, and it caught his accent.

Edward had grown solemn with the proximity of actual nuptials. She herself was nervous. At the Cana weekend a wife and mother Dolores's age embarrassed them all with a lot of personal stuff about how she enticed her husband, and women having to understand how frightened men are of intimacy.

"You were taught the opposite, right?" Her marble eyes were ringed by widened whites; her ringlets lay upon her forehead with a suggestion of sweat. Would she talk about positions next?

Instead she talked about the fact that, marriage or not, from time to time one felt attracted to another man. This happens. It doesn't mean the marriage is over. It's natural.

"I'm not saying give in," she said, smiling wickedly.

"Have you ever?" a voice asked, heavy with a sarcasm she missed.

"I can't answer with him in the room." "Him" was her balding husband, whose compensatory sideburns were so thin they needed fertilizer. While she babbled, he had been lounging a little upstage, arms folded, legs crossed, a false smile pasted on his chapped lips. Now he glared at his wife with real hatred. Hadn't the phrase "role models" been used when these two were introduced?

Edward sat beside her, frozen with embarrassment. Vera put a hand on his and looked at him, eyes rolling heavenward. He gave her a sickly smile. Maybe it was part of a test, to see if they really wanted to get married. Vera had a sudden memory of Andrea as a brand-new nun, all aglow with self-denial. Though he slay me, yet will I love him. Finally the woman waddled offstage, and her husband followed a few feet behind. The brides- and grooms-to-be looked around, avoiding eye contact, then left the auditorium.

The Cana weekend was held in a Catholic high school, but their rooms were booked in a nearby hotel someone had bequeathed to the archdiocese. Narrow corridors, dark wood, the light fixtures metallic ornamental flowers sprouting forty-watt bulbs. There was a transom over the narrow door to each room, and a vent in the lower panel. Edward walked her to her door. His room was next to hers. Was this another test? But the thought of doing anything other than sleeping in that hotel made her dizzy. Besides, Edward had not sought to go beyond a passionate kiss. He gave her one now, more prolonged than usual, perhaps egged on by the memory of the awful woman's words.

She unlocked the door, and they looked in at the room from the hall. The bed seemed unusually high, almost hospital height, lifting the eye to the wooden rail that ran around the four walls of the room a foot below the ceiling. An overstuffed chair with a floor lamp that seemed to be looking over its shoulder, a metal beaded chain dangling from its paneled shade. There was no television. There was no radio. As it turned out, there was not even a Gideon Bible.

Why such detail? Why did she remember as clearly as her name the way the cracked ceiling had suggested the map of Wisconsin? Because, looking up at it, lying in Edward's arms, she had located Madison and Superior and Hudson, across from the Twin Cities, and Milwaukee.

"Isn't that where your friend the nun lived?"

She had told him about Andrea; she had told him about everything. She nodded. He had hair on his chest, and at that exact moment she did not know whether she liked it or not.

"The Bride of Christ."

That was the phrase. Our Lord as husband, the nun as spiritual spouse. Consecrated virginity. Nothing in Vera's Catholic upbringing could soften the shock of such talk. Reading Andrea's letter—four pages, each single sheet folded once, JMJ (or Jesus, Mary, and Joseph) at the top of each, the elegant, spidery scrawl, fountain pen, not ballpoint—in which such lore was contained, Vera, child of the century, could not help seeing it all in pop-Freudian terms. Suppression, sublimation, a bow and a tip of the Hatlo hat to the view that sex is at the bottom of everything. The Church is the Bride of Christ; Christ comes to each soul as a lover to his beloved. Andrea quoted Saint Paul. She cited the Song of Songs. The Song of Songs! Vera read it—for the first time; she had been raised a Catholic and got such Scripture as she did mainly at Mass—and was hard put to see a spiritual dimension to the heated text, prose or poetry, it was hard to say. Lying in Edward's arms in that awful bed in that awful room on that awful weekend, sinfully anticipating the intimacies of marriage, she decided that, remorse and the wish that they hadn't done it aside, she preferred the literal to the metaphorical in these matters.

"I've never known any nuns," Edward said, moving her head higher on his arm. "My arm's going to sleep."

"It's got more brains than we do."

"Vera, I'm sorry . . ."

She put a finger to his lips and shook her head. They could feel contrition later. "Didn't you have nuns in school?"

His parish had not had a school. "We were lucky to have a priest. Did you ever think of becoming one?"

"A nun?"

His cheek moved against her head. A nod. It seemed an odd question in the circumstances. They had pulled the sheet up to her chin and his nipples. Beneath it they looked like a Flemish master's version of Adam and Eve, she apple-breasted, dimpled-bellied, wide-hipped, he angulary, sinewy, hirsute, his manhood flaccid in repose. Thank God there had been no Arthurian whining when, rampant, he had taken her. And now, staring at a cracked Wisconsin and its imaginary Milwaukee, he wondered if she had ever wanted to be a nun. She moved her head slowly from side to side.

In that weird way Andrea was involved in their marriage from the beginning. Just as, thanks to letters, Vera had felt part of Andrea's profession. At the outset of the ceremony, she had worn the dress her mother wore at her wedding; at a certain point she withdrew and, with the help of her sisters in religion, donned the habit. Her return to the chapel was dramatic. Her mother wept, her father wept, Charlotte wept. Andrea described herself as happy beyond belief, though of course there are some things that lie beyond the power of words to tell. The suggestion was of a forceful spiritual experience, a sense of union with Jesus in the manner suggested by the imagery.

Vera had had to read such letters a bit at a time, fascinated, angry, saddened, happy for her friend, but they were like news from the Middle Ages. If she was surprised, what would the vast majority of people think to find that this sort of thing was going on all around them, not only in Milwaukee, everywhere? No wonder she would lend Andrea a sympathetic ear when, some years later, come to Chicago, a vision in polka dots, she talked of updating the religious vocation and getting the nun into contact with the world around her.

Vera did not borrow a dress for her wedding day. In fitted, flowing white silk that traced the still-perfect lines of her body and culminated in supererogatory swirls that lay upon the altar steps like Dali watches, in a lace-brimmed picture hat, holding a single rose, she looked into the camera with the serene expression of a woman who has found her purpose in life. Framed, this picture stood upon the grand piano in the living room for years, and Vera would often take it in her hands to study it, to consult her own face for clues to the meaning of life.

95

The only wisdom not suggested in the photograph was the carnal knowledge she had acquired with Edward on their Cana weekend.

It was not yet midnight when Edward, dressed even to the point of wearing his tie, had left her room and gone to his own and she was left with her thoughts. A consciousness of having sinned was not prominent among them. After all, she and Edward intended to marry. In a sense, that is what they had done tonight, a private ceremony before the public. Marriage is a sacrament conferred by the participants, not the priest. She remembered that much of her catechism. The priest confers the blessing of the Church on the happy couple. Vera decided it was a marriage ceremony, not premarital sex, that had occurred in her narrow bed.

Even so, neither she nor Edward received Holy Communion the next day. Just as well, since two weeks later, when they went to confession at the cathedral, the confessor did not accept her version of what they had done.

"Has this continued?"

"No, Father." No need to add that they hadn't had the opportunity.

"See that it doesn't. Wait till after the wedding. Can you do that?"

"Yes, Father."

And they did. Would they have anticipated their marital rights at all if it had not been for that dreadful hotel?

Later, when it occurred to Vera to ask herself if that stolen pleasure in a hotel bed had affected her marriage adversely, she could not bring herself to think so. It was the talk about Andrea, rather than the lovely, awkward sex, that seemed ominous in that episode.

5·

Dolores, matron of honor at the wedding, continued as confidante and mentor. Edward and Howard got along famously, their closeness clouded only slightly when Edward bought the boat, thus drawing attention to the fact that a dentist with only a wife has it all over even a supersalesman with a wife, five children, and bills, bills, bills.

"Wait to have children," Dolores advised.

Vera raised her brow and glanced across the room to where Katy played.

"I'm not saying don't have any. Have those you have. But put it off."

"We'll see."

"We'll see? If that's the best you can do, we'll see all right. You can use the pill, you know. It's all right. My confessor tells me that. *Now* he tells me that." Dolores lifted her eyes to heaven. It occurred to Vera that Dolores had not been pregnant for some time. Had she thought Howard had lost interest?

"I feel I've already put it off."

"At twenty-four?"

"I am twenty-five," Vera corrected. "How many children did you have when you were twenty-five?"

"I'll tell you when I get there."

Dolores was eleven years her sister's senior.

The boat, a twenty-three-foot sloop, was called *Whoops* when they bought her, but they renamed her the *Dental Flaws*, bought new rigging, had the inboard overhauled, and spent as much of the first summer of their marriage aboard her as they could. Dentists have no homework, of course, but Vera promoted the fiction that she got lots of work done in the diminutive cabin. She did bring a briefcase aboard, but from then on it was a matter of keeping it dry rather than opening it. They crewed well together, she and Edward, taking turns at the helm, seldom using the automatic, reveling in the Lake Michigan wind in their sails and the midwestern sun burning the skin off their noses. A typical weekend involved sailing to Benton Harbor, casting off in mid-afternoon Friday if they could manage, or at the crack of dawn on Saturday. They would head out of Belmont Harbor and watch the marvel of the Chicago skyline establish itself and then fade in the distance. Edward would have carefully charted the course, they had radio and radar, they were seldom out of sight of land, but sailing was an adventure nonetheless.

They would dine ashore and spend the night on board. Then out again the following morning for a great, looping return to Chicago. Vera covered her face with cream and wore broad-brimmed hats to protect herself from the sun and the even more relentless wind. Even so she ended up with very dry, very tan skin, the mark of her sunglasses giving her a sort of raccoon look ashore. Edward took no precautions, reveling in wind and sun, unmindful of the leathery look his face took on. Vera liked his sailor's squint, the competence with which he handled the boat, the ease with which he assumed she was more than crew enough for him. She had thought of the boat as a compensatory toy when Edward bought it, and it did make up for, or at least enable him to forget, what they did not have. Vera did not for long feel condescending about Edward's need to ready the boat, maneuver it through the harbor, hoist sail after they cleared the breakwater, master of his vessel, of its crew, and so, at least for the length of a voyage, of his life. She needed the boat herself as time went on. It was a little world in which she and Edward were complete, no need to brood on what they did not have.

He took it well enough, their not having children, and thereby gained stature in her eyes. Wasn't it for him that she wanted to have a baby? It was only natural that he should want a child. But he never complained. He shared her concern—how could he not?—but it was *their* problem, not *hers,* and that meant more than she realized at the time. Edward was good with kids. A sizable percentage of his patients were children. At the marina he was always showing kids how to sail Lasers, and even entered the annual August Laser race. Watching him move out to a commanding lead, Vera sometimes felt she was cheering on a son as much as a husband. Twice Edward threw the race, letting a kid get past him when Vera knew he could have held the lead. That somehow summed him up. If he could seem like a kid himself, he always ended by establishing his maturity.

The boat as much as anything explained how going to weekly Mass fell into desuetude for them, yet Vera felt close to God on his water, under his sky, conscious of the smallness of their craft and the unpredictability of the weather. Besides, they never made a decision not to go to Mass. Nor was anyone pushing the obligation in those days. When they did go, the ritual was often unrecognizable. Edward did not like women reading the scriptures to him from the pulpit, and Vera found it impossible to defend the practice.

She made the mistake of saying this to Andrea during one of her visits. Now that Andrea was studying theology at the University of Chicago, they saw more of one another. Vera should have known what her old friend's reaction would be. Wearing white slacks and an orange warm-up jacket string-tied well below her hips, her toes asserting themselves from her sandals (the only Franciscan suggestion in her clothing), Andrea sat beside Vera on deck with the Chicago skyline altering gyroscopically in the background and then moving slowly westward as the *Dental Flaws* turned on its line in a freshet of wind.

"Women will be ordained, Vera."

"God forbid."

"I'm serious."

And she was. This was the first appearance of Andrea the feminist, and it was a crucial development. She had earned her master's at Marquette and come to Chicago just before the opening of classes.

It was the academic year that continued to measure Andrea's days. When she had written to say she would be coming for the beginning of the year, she meant early September.

"There'll be lots of good sailing left."

Sitting on the deck of the *Dental Flaws,* Andrea looked around at the other boats. Far out on the lake, small white triangles blended in the haze of light where sky and spangled water met. Andrea lifted a hand to shade her eyes.

"Let me get you a pair of sunglasses."

"Do you have an extra pair of shorts on board?"

"There are some spare swimsuits."

Vera chased Edward from the cabin, where he was working on his ship-to-shore, so that Andrea could change. She changed in the head, a trick in itself, but boating makes its demands on the modest. Edward had gone forward to the bow to check the pulpit storage. Vera had gone back to the blanket she had spread out on the deck for Andrea and herself. Edward glanced over his shoulder, then, still crouched, turned slowly. The expression on his face was comic.

Andrea had come up from the cabin and was standing with one hand on a guy line, the other shielding her eyes, looking out over the lake. She was a sight to behold. The suit, a faded blue one, was too small, the lower part hardly more than a loincloth. No halter would have confined Andrea's breasts, but this one scarcely made her presentable. Or too presentable.

She turned and, apparently unaware of the impression she had made on Edward, rejoined Vera on the deck.

"Drinks?" Edward said, then cleared his throat and repeated it. He sounded as if his voice were changing.

"Nothing for me, dear." She almost never called Edward "dear."

"Tell me you don't have gin and tonic," Andrea said.

"I'd only be lying. Sure you won't have one, Vere?" Edward slapped her bottom as he went by. That was something he never did. They both seemed suddenly eager to let Andrea know that they were husband and wife, that they enjoyed unspeakable intimacies together and self-control sometimes was difficult, even in company.

"A light one."

Andrea sighed. "It seems almost a sin to be on a boat like this."

"Sometimes it is."

Andrea just looked at her. "Last year I worked with people in Milwaukee who had no idea such things exist."

"Milwaukee is a big boating town."

"Not for these people."

"Are you suggesting we sell our boat and give the proceeds to the poor?"

"Only if you put it off until tomorrow." She looked down her long body, untanned but not the fish-belly white Vera's was at the beginning of summer. "This suit hardly covers me."

"What does it matter out here?"

"I guess you're right. But I don't want to embarrass Edward."

Embarrass Edward? "Don't worry. I put saltpeter in our water supply."

Andrea did not understand. She insisted on an explanation. What is deader than an explained joke? An unembarrassed Edward arrived with the drinks.

"I'm having rum and Coke," he announced.

"Yo ho ho."

"My father was a dentist," Andrea said, having tasted her drink. With the tip of her tongue, she captured an effervescent bubble on her upper lip.

"That's what Vera tells me."

Andrea herself had told him this on at least two previous occasions, dropping the remark at a time when it
could not be followed up, had Edward been so inclined.
But he had been far less interested in Andrea when she
was dressed. Perhaps the cross around her neck, or the
enameled pin, or whatever symbol was meant to suggest her vocation, was an anaphrodisiac then. Anyone
who could think of this full-bodied woman with all her
wares on display as a nun would have to swear off
Boccaccio.

"He died in his office."

"With his boots on?"

Andrea rested her glass against her lower lip, looking beyond Edward at the water. Vera had given Edward
none of the details on the death of Dr. Bauer. She did
not even know if Andrea knew them all.

"I guess you could say that."

Vera had heard the story from Charlotte, not understanding why anyone would want to pass on such dreadful details about her own father.

"Because I don't blame him, not really. My mother
shut him off, so what was he supposed to do. Make a
novena? Pornography is a way of being faithful, when
you stop to think of it. Oh, he had tried infidelity, too.
I don't blame him for that either. But imagine, a man
his age, making love to a balloon woman for God's sake."

Vera could not imagine it. Nor did she try particularly
hard. She had always liked Dr. Bauer. But her liking
him could not survive her conversation with Charlotte.

"Of course my mother thinks he went straight to
hell."

"Did she say that?"

"She didn't have to."

Now, aboard the *Dental Flaws*, at anchor in Belmont Harbor, Andrea took the glass from her lip and asked Edward what it was like to practice in Chicago.

It might have been the first time Vera had heard her husband describe his professional life. She knew all the details, of course, but the narrative turned him briefly into a stranger, a man reducible to the life he was now describing. She looked for a negative reaction when Edward indicated vaguely that his was a lucrative practice and growing more so every year.

"Hence the boat?"

Edward smiled.

"And the Jaguar?"

"Never trust a dentist."

"I'll remember that."

Of Andrea, Edward said little when he and Vera were alone. "Would you know she's a nun?" Vera asked.

He laughed. And that was before he had seen her in a bathing suit. Vera herself could not find much of the nun Andrea had been, and after that first visit to the boat, she began to think it was only a matter of time before Andrea realized she had effectively left the convent.

"Edward's nice," Andrea had said after she first met him. After the visit to the boat, over coffee on the University of Chicago campus, Andrea said, "He's changed."

"In what way?"

"He seems older."

"He is. We all are."

Andrea nodded in agreement, but Vera could see she did not really believe it of herself.

PART FOUR

The Lawyer and the Nun

I.

As a delegate to the convention of the order held the summer after her father died, Andrea had sided with the dwindling band that resisted change. That the habit she had so recently put on should be cast aside for the hybrid outfit proposed was unthinkable. The new costume looked like something doodled up in haste rather than a carefully considered alternative.

"Of course it's only the first step," Sister Margaret Mary warned. A former superior, she was seventy, with clear, translucent skin and eyes serene from accepting the fact that she was dying of cancer. "Next will go the veil, and soon any semblance of distinctive garb."

Andrea felt threatened and cheated, as if everything she had left the world for was in danger of being stolen from her.

The majority argued that they were simply implementing the directives of the council. Vatican II called on religious communities to act more effectively in the world. It was accepted as axiomatic that the traditional habit was an obstacle to the work of the nun. If people were not put off by wimples and veils, they would be more at ease with religious women.

"It is not the comfort of the laity that is behind this proposal," Sister Margaret Mary told the assembly. "It is our own. We want to fuss over clothes again. The argument used on behalf of a new habit could be used as easily on behalf of wearing makeup."

This had drawn polite but derisive laughter. What a prophet the old nun had been. Mercifully, she had not lived long enough to see her predictions come true. And they did come true, except in one particular. When the time came that nuns were using makeup, it was no longer necessary to devise complex arguments in its favor. Change soon gained such momentum that it swept everything before it. Including Andrea. But at the beginning she had resisted, allying herself with Sister Margaret Mary, only to see every motion she favored go down to defeat in the voting.

"You mustn't let it upset you," Sister Margaret Mary had said, taking her hand. "And you must be strong. The time is coming when a serious religious will be as odd within the convent as we all now seem to the world at large. Be true to your vocation, Sister Duns Scotus."

Andrea had wept when Sister Margaret Mary died. With the venerable old nun died anything like a dissident—that is, traditionalist—faction. Andrea found her own resolution weakening and the day soon came when she hoped others would not remember the positions she had taken at the assembly. For a time she felt like Saint Peter, dreading the occasion when she must deny her past adherence. She had recognized the need for change, but still she feared her former conservatism would be held against her. The crucial point was reached when she asked permission to apply to graduate schools.

"Did you have some place special in mind, Sister Andrea?" Sister Jeanne asked.

The superior was no longer called "Mother," and they had all dropped the names given them at profession and reverted to their baptismal names. Andrea could not honestly say she missed being addressed as Duns Scotus. Sister Jeanne, the new superior, had neither the autocratic aloofness of her predecessor nor the sugary, nunnish deference instilled by the traditional novitiate. Andrea had the feeling that if she made a good case, she would get a favorable judgment.

"I'd like to go to Marquette."

"Why?"

Andrea mentioned what she had heard of the theology department there, the daring and innovation, the controversies that seemed to go right to the heart of current questions. Jeanne perked up at the mention of fellowships.

"Andrea, if you get a fellowship, if you can support yourself, of course you can go."

It had not occurred to Andrea that the decision would turn on money. That this had not occurred to her seemed a measure of what was wrong with convent life as she had known it. How naively unaware she was of what would be self-evident to anyone else. Permission of her superiors would scarcely put food in her mouth or a roof over her head, and provisions for those had to come from somewhere.

She applied for and got the graduate fellowship. By sharing an apartment with two other nuns, she was more than able to take care of herself. On the practical side alone, the years in Milwaukee matured her, made her more self-sufficient, gave her a better sense of the problems faced by the vast majority of people. Money problems. But the theoretical changes wrought by the graduate study of theology were far more profound.

The nuns she lived with were from different orders, and that was an enlarging experience, too. Alma belonged to the order founded by Mother Elizabeth Seton, Mary Agnes to the Dominicans. The funny thing was that their communities had gone through exactly the same wrenching changes Andrea's had, except that Alma and Mary Agnes had been all for them from the start. Mary Agnes had pictures of herself in the old Dominican habit, and she looked wonderful in it, chastely white and black. The outfits she now wore did little to conceal the fact that she was fifty pounds overweight and had shapeless legs. The truth was, she had no clothes sense at all. But she was easily the brightest of the three. Alma was a strawberry blonde reminiscent of a Botticelli Madonna. Her peering, near-sighted expression added a twinkle to her eyes, and she looked at you as if she had just blown away a strand of hair. In her reactions to their courses, Andrea could see her own mirrored in undissembled fashion.

"I wouldn't want my mother to hear that," Alma said when they were taking a course on the composition of the New Testament.

"I wouldn't want my mother to hear that" became their byword for anything that went contrary to the traditional understanding of the faith. There was something of an in-group attitude in the graduate program, Andrea thought. Theologians were engaged in a long and almost surreptitious rewriting of the tenets of Catholicism, prompted to do so by Vatican II, of course, and there was a constant awareness of unnamed enemies of the effort. For those in catechetics, it was the parents. Teachers of children had to be prepared for negative reactions from parents and pastors. Theologians had to be cautious not to run afoul of the old guard among the bishops. "I wouldn't want my mother to hear that." These were the growing pains of the new Church.

Not that theoretical topics dominated. In those days there was the overwhelming fact of the war and the need to speak out against it. Justice and Peace took precedence over everything else.

"Orthopraxy is at least as important as orthodoxy."

That sentence, written in Andrea's notebook, was to become her personal motto, although her first irrelevant reaction to it had been to think of orthodontics, her father, and other somber matters. What would her own mother have made of the new theology? Since Mrs. Bauer's knowledge of the old was not abstract, the contrast could not have struck her. It was Vera, oddly enough, who proved to be reactionary.

"Vera, I know exactly how you feel. I felt the same way."

"And you got over it?"

"That's right."

"Have you any idea how condescending that sounds?"

No more than she felt?

Her letters to Vera had been on occasion a reworking of lecture notes, putting it all into her own words for the benefit of an intelligent, educated laywoman. But Vera had an annoying habit of reacting negatively to precisely the things she was supposed to find attractive—supposed to, that is, if she were a good example of the intelligent, educated laywoman. This was even truer when they got together and spoke face to face than it was in their letters.

Andrea would have thought her letters had prepared Vera for the way she was dressed the first time she went down to Chicago to see her old friend, but obviously they had not, and it was only ambiguously pleasant to be fussed over so much. Vera's manner might have indicated suppressed disapproval. Not that Andrea was unaware of how stunning she looked in the polka-dot dress. "Wow," Alma said when she emerged from the dressing room at the Shape Shoppe on Wisconsin Avenue, and "Wow," said Vera when they met in the lobby of the Palmer House. Vera spoke before stepping off the escalator, and her remark turned a few heads, adding to Andrea's ambiguous pleasure. The ambiguity began when Vera said, a trifle loudly, "Sister, you look lovely."

And Vera, on subjects of controversy, did sound almost exactly as she herself had when she was the junior ally of Sister Margaret Mary.

"I'm sorry, Andrea, but I don't get it. What's the point of being a nun if you dress like everyone else, live like everyone else, and make your living like everyone else?"

"We are the new nuns, Vera. With a new mission to the world today, not the world of centuries ago, when our orders were founded. We have all been rethinking our aims, referring to the idea our founders had, adapting that idea . . ."

Vera wasn't really listening. "And now you just apply for jobs?"

"Well, I want my doctorate first."

"More study?"

"I'll be coming to Chicago."

She had been accepted in theology, but her intention was to concentrate on psychology. Her eyes had been opened by a course she had taken at the University of Wisconsin Milwaukee campus. Fueled by talk of justice and peace, she wanted to help people as never before, but what did she really know about people, about what made them tick or how to implement change? All she had to do was frame the questions to know the depressing answer.

Vera did not exactly toast the idea of Andrea's coming to Chicago, and for the first time Andrea admitted to herself that there had always been an unconscious rivalry between them. Her vocation had been a gain for her, a loss for Vera, suggesting as it did that she had the deeper notion of what life was all about. She could finally admit that she had half feared her entering the convent would put the idea into Vera's head. How could anyone fail to feel the attraction of the religious life? Now both her growing maturity and her graduate work were points in this unacknowledged contest. On the other hand, Vera was a lawyer, working with a good firm. And wondering how Andrea the nun's life differed from her own.

"Because we're both single?"

"I won't be for long."

She had to coax it out of Vera, that afternoon in the Palmer House, which was a bit annoying given how frank she herself had been. Vera wore a tailored Oxford gray suit with an organdy blouse, and she was holding a breadstick horizontally beneath her eyes, index fingers pressing its ends. She seemed to be measuring Andrea.

To see if she were on the level? In any case, the man's name was Edward.

"He's a dentist."

Andrea returned her wine glass carefully to the table, half expecting Vera to say it, but she didn't so Andrea did, exorcising the subject.

"Like my father."

"There the similarity ends," Vera said, too quickly, and then there was an embarrassing silence during which Andrea wondered how much Vera knew about the circumstances of her father's death.

"Is it official?"

For answer Vera extended her hand. Good Lord, she should have noticed the ring; Vera had been doing everything but pushing it under her nose since they sat down. Was it large or small? Andrea could not say. As its significance dawned on her, she leaned toward Vera and could not keep the tears from her eyes.

"I'm so happy for you." She remembered how Vera had reacted to the notion of the nun as the Bride of Christ. "So you will be the bride of Edward."

"His love, his dove."

"His beautiful one," Andrea added. And Vera did look beautiful, a woman in love.

2.

Their first apartment was on the near north side, convenient to Edward's office as well as her own; he went north on Lake Shore Drive each morning, and

she went south. The second Sunday after they were
married, they went to his office so that he could
show her around unimpeded by nurses and patients.
He put her into his chair, checked her teeth, and
found them all but perfect. She refused to have X rays
taken.

In return she devised a program so that he could
computerize the paperwork for his practice. This entailed bringing in a new girl who was not overawed by
the computer and easing out a receptionist who had
been with him since he opened the office. Herb Rosner,
his accountant, appreciated the system more than Edward did.

"You adapt some software, or is this your own program?" he asked Vera.

"It's my own."

Herb's glasses might have been prescribed to correct
his cheekbones. He never seemed to look directly
through them.

"Market it. Edward's colleagues give you a natural
clientele. Not that you'd have to be a dentist or a doctor to find it useful."

Shrewd little Herb. Vera registered the copyright,
wrote a manual, circulated a letter to the city's dentists.
She put an eight hundred dollar price on it and had
sold a thousand before she was approached by Byttner
Software, a national concern. Eventually their offer was
irresistible, a quarter of a million dollars, payable over
five years, and a ten percent royalty on each program
sold. It was a relief to get rid of what had begun as a
cottage industry and ended by taking up a good deal
too much of her time. But it was this personal experi-

ence that made her particularly aware of the legal ramifications of the computer revolution.

How to copyright a product that could be so easily copied? Leasing or licensing rather than selling outright, with embedded codes that rendered the software inoperative after a given date, helped to get around that but created additional problems when more than the program itself was destroyed. The main relief Vera felt in selling to Byttner was getting rid of the specter of litigation. But she brought Byttner's business to Patterson, Patterson, Flood and Barrett, and the account of course became hers. Although still a junior partner, she was, five years out of law school, in a position to retire if she wanted to. What she wanted was a family.

They both wanted a family. It began as a natural expectation, turned to mild surprise when nothing happened, and evolved into a conscious project that occupied them for years. To say that spontaneity suffered would be a wild understatement. Vera would emerge from the bathroom and slip into bed beside Edward with the annoying thought that their lovemaking was an exercise in scientific breeding. There were thermometers, charts, half a dozen surefire systems, physical exams—everything but a baby.

It wasn't that they weren't relaxed with one another. Edward had been less than adept the first time, on their Cana weekend, but it was an eager, not a nervous, clumsiness. Quite soon they were fully at ease with one another. Everything was right. And still there was no baby.

These things happen, doctors said. Give it time.

Relax.

They were told that often, relax, and the suggestion was that some psychological hang-up prevented them from letting themselves go and really enjoying themselves. It was hard to deny that, as the years went by without her becoming pregnant, sex lost its first allure. It became a chore. It became something which, however successful and satisfying the act, was nonetheless a failure.

In the wake of *Roe* vs. *Wade*, as many as a million and a half babies were aborted every year, but Vera could not get pregnant. There were hundreds of unwanted kids in Chicago, admittedly most of them were black, yet she and Edward, for all their desire, could not have a child.

Adoption? The one time she approached the subject, Edward winced as if she had struck him.

"It happens all the time. No sooner does a couple adopt a child than the wife gets pregnant with her own."

"Then they must have been doing something wrong," he said, and he sounded as if he were holding his breath and talking at the same time.

The suggestion that they, particularly he, might be inadequate in the sexual department was intolerable to Edward. It didn't make her heart leap either. And Edward was right. There was nothing they had not done; they had become quite expert at lovemaking, not that she took much pride in that. It was a sterile expertise.

Finally Vera had the ultimate physical and learned that there was nothing wrong with her. She was, in the odd analogy of the young doctor, sound as a dollar.

So it had to be Edward.

The realization filled her with a new tenderness toward him.

To take his mind off what they did not have, Vera encouraged him to buy things.

He had a powerful ham radio station built in the basement of the house they bought in Evanston. With an eye to buying a plane, they took flying lessons, but a bad scare when they were caught in a sudden rainstorm deflected them before the purchase was made. Racquet ball, tennis, swimming. They were both in marvelous shape. Several friends had boats, and they crewed from time to time, but their intention to buy their own had, for a time, been opposed by those who had them.

"A boat is a hole in the water down which you shovel money."

"The two happiest days of your life are, first, when you buy a boat, and second, when you sell it."

As an instance of postponed gratification, the boat was that much more delightful when finally they bought it.

They got used to having Andrea in Chicago. After that first afternoon on the *Dental Flaws*, she was liable to telephone at any time, at home or at the office.

When she called Edward at the office, it was to make an appointment.

Vera discovered that the thought of Andrea in Edward's chair was both welcome and unwelcome. Edward's joke that he looked forward to seeing her with her mouth open yet unable to talk, was one he had used too many times before. Surely there must be something unattractive about anyone from the dentist's point of view. But then she remembered those stories about Andrea's father. Finally she laughed away her reaction. Good grief, you would think she was jealous of Andrea. Jealous of a nun.

Unfortunately the term "nun" conjured up the image of a wizened little lady all got up in voluminous skirts, starched wimple, and god-awful headdress. Even before Andrea's order had gone on the flake, she hadn't looked like that, but now, even on what had to be a limited budget, Andrea managed to look like a million dollars.

"Well, how does she look?"

Edward, pitching his hat onto the upper shelf of the hall closet, looked at her blankly.

"Is she riddled with cavities, in danger of pyorrhea, will a denture be needed?"

"Andrea? You're not even close."

"Ah, but you were. Tell me about it."

Andrea, nearly thirty, had decided to have a slight overbite corrected, and Edward had referred her to an orthodontist.

"Braces!"

"They're not as complicated as they used to be. Nor as visible."

"Edward, even if she had buck teeth, and she doesn't, she's a *nun*."

"That doesn't mean she shouldn't look her best."

"She looks just fine the way she is."

"If she can have cavities filled, why can't she have a better bite?"

Who had thought of that argument, Andrea or Edward? Vera didn't care. She thought such vanity in a nun was inexcusable.

3.

Andrea felt like a fool during the months her teeth were being straightened. She had to remember not to smile. When she forgot, one glimpse of her teeth turned even the nicest people nasty.

Alma had recently left her order and was staying with Andrea in Oak Park, looking and acting like a waif, in her early thirties and lost. With twice the brains of most people, she had only half the practical sense. She had had no practice. In many ways she was still a girl. When she saw the metal and rubber-band monstrosity that Andrea's mouth had become, she clapped a hand over her own, but could not stifle a helpless giggle.

"Thanks," Andrea said.

"Oh, I'm sorry, Andrea, I truly am," Alma apologized, clinging to her arm and preventing her from leaving the room. "Are those braces?"

"Look, it is ridiculous, I admit it. I am indulging my vanity. But the die is cast, and I really do not regret it. When I was little, I pleaded with my father to let me have my teeth corrected, but he always refused."

"But what's wrong with your teeth?"

"Alma, don't pretend. They hang over my chin."

"You have perfect teeth!"

How could she stay angry at Alma? The apartment on Austin Avenue in Oak Park had two bedrooms, was in an integrated neighborhood, faced the street. The kitchen was comically small, the dining room one a chatelaine could have loved, and the furnishings were minimal: apple crate, Goodwill, and beanbag. It was the first place Andrea had had all to herself. Here at last she felt like an adult. She was happy to take Alma in and listen to her cry her way into full adjustment to her new status.

"Andrea, the worst part is, there is no change. I mean, what's so different? In the old days I would have put off the habit and had to buy new clothes. I would have had to get used to the world outside the convent. Who lives inside anymore? Do any of you?"

Any members of her order. "Some."

"The halt and the lame."

"More or less." The faculty at their college in Green Bay was largely lay now; the president was a layman.

"Andrea, how has my life changed since I withdrew from the order?"

"Aren't you emphasizing superficial things?"

Alma looked appropriately sheepish, pouting prettily. She wore an oversized puffy white sweatshirt and jeans that seem pasted to her legs. The red mules were Andrea's and comically large. Andrea wished she were as impressed by her answer as Alma seemed to be.

Andrea was on the mailing list of her order and received several pieces of mail a week, for the most part impersonal. Sister Jeanne had left, eloping with the comptroller of the college, who left behind a distraught wife and two children in high school. It seemed a sign of the times that no one really was shocked. Such defections had been occurring for years now, and if at first they had been newsworthy, they no longer qualified as stop-the-press scandals. The absconded couple were headed for California, where Jeanne hoped to open a counseling office.

"You could do that yourself, couldn't you?" Alma asked.

"Run away with a comptroller?"

Alma made a face. Could she do anything that would diminish her prettiness? "Couldn't you open a counseling service?"

"I would have to get an Illinois license."

"Is that hard?"

Not hard at all. Andrea mentioned it to Vera and within a week had a letter from one of her colleagues at Patterson, Patterson, Flood and Barrett outlining the procedure. Vera shook her head when Andrea asked what the fee was.

"Part of our service to nuns."

Andrea filed away the information on how to become a licensed psychological counselor.

"Your turn to make dinner," she reminded Alma.

"I'm going to take you out."

"You can't afford it."

"I can, too." While she had any money at all, Alma felt solvent. Sufficient for the day . . . Once her attitude might have indicated an edifying trust in divine providence. Was it still that or just ordinary irresponsibility?

"Well, I don't want to eat out with my mouth looking like this."

"No one will notice."

"You did."

"That's different. How long do you have to keep those . . ." She settled for pointing, not wanting to risk a description.

They went out to dinner. Alma's question had indicated how silly it was to think she could hide for the better part of a year.

That was in the fall, late September. Throughout that year Andrea took classes, did some interning with outpatients, was checked by the orthodontist regularly, and kept her appointments with Edward.

They were more like dates. She needed two fillings, and he did one per visit, finishing in ten or fifteen minutes and then spending the rest of the half hour chatting with her. His usual procedure was to handle two patients more or less simultaneously, going from one to the other. His dental technician made this doubling of income possible. But he never made use of Noreen when Andrea was there. And of course he checked on the orthodonture as well.

"He should take that stuff out of there pretty soon."

"He hasn't given me a date."

"I hope not." Joking was part of Edward's chairside manner. "A retainer will be plenty in a few weeks."

He was right. But she came back again to Edward, who wanted to buff the fillings and do a little cleaning work. Knowing that he was doing it as a favor, Andrea could scarcely say no.

Edward wore powder blue high-collared coats in the office, gray flannels, loafers with the nicest mahogany shine. He had a way of tipping his head as if listening to his own thoughts before expressing them. A very restful conversationalist, reassuring. But on the topic of the boat, he got almost excited.

Things. Possessions. Consumerism. Vera and Edward were textbook instances of the pointless accumulation of luxuries. Andrea enjoyed feeling superior to Vera and Edward. She herself, after all, had taken the vow of poverty. She found that she preferred the ragtag look of her apartment in Oak Park to the Sybaritic comfort of the house in Evanston, where she was always welcome. Everything was in exquisite taste, no ostentation, each object specially chosen. It was Edward who leaned in the direction of the showy. He was inordinately proud of his shortwave radio and, more recently, of the personal computer on which Vera was giving him instruction. If there was one indulgence Andrea envied, it was the flying lessons.

"I wish you had bought a plane."

"Planes can be rented."

"Do you ever rent one?"

"Would you like to go up?"

"Are you serious?"

Edward was serious if she was. And so, on the following Wednesday, she was strapped into a seat beside him and they took off in an unbelievably small Cessna from Meigs Field, lifting right out over the water in a way that lifted her heart and made her stomach sink. She actually cried out with excitement.

At the controls of the aircraft, Edward was a changed man, confident, expert, calm. A small smile greeted her cry, but he was too busy at the time to do more. Within minutes Andrea had lost all sense of speed, at least when she looked up or straight ahead. They rose toward the clouds, and Andrea felt an almost spiritual ecstasy.

"Haven't you ever flown before?"

"No."

"I had no idea this was to be your maiden flight."

Andrea put her hand on his arm and smiled like a child.

4.

What percentage of the joy of sailing was anticipation? Poring over maps and charts, blocking off days on the calendar, laying in supplies, fussing over gear and canvas—Edward called it foreplay, but there was a sense in which the trips themselves were anticlimactic. Not the half-day, full-day sweeps out into the lake and back into their own harbor at nightfall; those were preparatory, too. Clearing the causeway knowing you would be returning that same day was a very different feeling from setting out on a sail that would last a week or more. Then, under way, the course set, settled in, the pace slackened and the Chicago skyline stood motionless to port.

Vera liked to make harbor in the early evening, tie up at an anchor buoy, and then row ashore in the dinghy for dinner. The restaurants in harbors were surprisingly good, or maybe their demands were less. Unadorned wideboard floors, the windowed walls giving a view of the lake as twilight gave way to night, a bottle of wine, Edward and herself.

"Happy?" he would ask.

"Mmmmm. You?"

Edward nodded. They seldom got more analytical

about themselves than that. Wife to his husband, Vera was content. That she knew many more intelligent men did not matter. Edward was solid and predictable and fun. He wore a Windbreaker, a captain's hat was on the floor beside his sneakered feet, his tan and his sun-bleached hair contributed to the nautical look. There was a pipe in his jacket pocket, one he had never smoked, quite obviously a prop, yet Vera approved without making fun of him even in the privacy of her own mind.

Under sail Edward was in charge. He was the captain, Vera the crew, and that carried over as long as they were in restaurants like the one in Saginaw where she had ordered lake trout and he the large bowl of chowder to be followed by a steak. The wine was local.

"Michigan wine?" Vera made a questioning frown.

"Didn't Hemingway write about it?"

The waitress seemed to be listening to some music inaudible to them. Her smile was vacant, suggestive of brain damage.

"Let's have a drink first."

Edward ordered rum and Coke. The girl looked dubious as she wrote it down. Vera asked for bourbon and water. Edward lit the candle when the girl went away: bulbous red glass enclosed in plastic mesh, its wick embedded in wax. Edward got it free and burned his fingers on the match, but soon it glowed between them like a twenty-four-hour vigil light.

"Make a wish, Edward."

"I've got my wish." His sneaker groped for hers.

Water is an aphrodisiac, a symbol of fertility. After eating they rowed back to the boat with a pleasant inner glow. Voices that carried over the smooth water of the harbor seemed uncannily close at hand, the sound of the oars' rhythmic progress mesmerizing. The complaint of the oarlock, the splash as the blade entered the water, the onward pull of the boat. Edward rowed well. He was also good at finding their boat in the dark.

They made love nightly when they slept aboard, lying scrunched together in a bunk, rocked gently by the tide as their own tempo quickened into a frenzied eagerness they never knew at home. Afterward they lay out on deck, under the stars, staring up at God and eternity, and Vera was certain she would become pregnant. The night sky was like a map of destiny, more impressive for her almost total inability to read it. Beside her Edward found stars and constellations, but for all she knew he was making them up.

Ursa Major, Ursa Minor, Dippers, all the rest. Vera looked up and saw sequins on black velvet or, more usually, the eye of God. Please let us have a baby. Let me be pregnant, please. She tried to think of things to promise in return, but the thought of bargaining with God reminded her of the spiritual bouquets they had prepared for their parents years ago, urged on by the nuns at school. Little handmade cards decorated with some symbol of the season, and inside, Masses 10, Rosaries 20, Visits to the Blessed Sacrament 6, Ejaculations 100. "My Jesus, mercy," was an ejaculation. These little bouquets had been likened by one nun to heavenly bankbooks, a little spiritual capital offered to their parents in return for all they had done for them.

The night sky could look close or far away; Vera did not know what made it seem either, but God seemed very near them as they lay on the deck of the *Dental*

Flaws, having made love, in awe of the stars. And Vera did bargain with God. I will attend daily Mass at St. Peter's downtown for a month (that entailed skipping lunch and thus had the added benefit of an enforced diet). I will recite the rosary—five decades—every day. I will send money to the missions. But, dear God, please let us have a baby.

But not even making love on board their boat nor keeping all those promises changed their luck. Vera had been amazed at the number of people who were in St. Peter's at midday. The confessionals in both side aisles did a brisk business, and on the high altar Mass succeeded Mass on the half hour. The clientele altered continuously, people coming and going, every conceivable type from the suavely prosperous to bag ladies who wrestled their sacks into a pew as they glared around at potential thieves. Vera had come to notice pregnant women, and there were many at those noontime Masses. Were they offering prayers of gratitude or praying for a safe delivery? Doubtless the latter. Who but she regarded getting pregnant as a feat?

They had been married three years when they bought the boat. They had been ready to start a family from the outset but had been putting their minds to it, so to speak, for a year and a half. The note of desperation had crept into bed with them.

Vera imagined that they were being punished for that Cana weekend, when they had made love under the cracked map of Wisconsin. But then she had imagined they were fulfilling their destiny when they made love under the starry skies of Lake Michigan and the watching eye of God. She was not good at reading signs, even those of her own body. Each month she charted and pursued the descent of the ova within her, and during the times of maximum vulnerability, she clung to Edward like an houri. If conceiving a child were a mental act, she would have borne quintuplets. Irrational as it was, she became angry at Edward.

During one of her ascetic bouts, undertaken to persuade God to let her get pregnant, Vera gave up smoking, wishing it were more difficult than it proved to be. The first day was one of light-headed nervousness; the second day she felt depressed, but it was a Saturday and she did not get out of bed until afternoon. On the Sunday she told herself that if she got through this third day, it would be enough. But on Monday she simply failed to smoke. She felt no desire to, so she didn't. For the rest of the week, she said nothing to anybody, believing that she would soon be overwhelmed by a desire to light up. The desire never came. On the second weekend she told Edward she had quit.

"Good luck."

"Edward, I quit a week ago. More than a week ago."

He was assembling a television set he had bought as a kit from some mail-order place in Michigan. He smiled, tilting his head, half closing one eye. He might have been protecting it from the smoke that lifted from the cigarette smoldering in the tray on his workbench.

"Come on."

"Edward, I'm serious. Have you seen me smoke one cigarette this past week?"

He had not noticed. She could not believe it. But then she had not noticed when Gerry Flood had grown a mustache. She was as peeved as her office colleague had been. Edward could not possibly have failed to notice she was not smoking.

"If you say so."

"Do you know what the joke is? It's easy to stop. It really and truly is. I thought it would be terrible, and it wasn't."

She became a missionary. Edward had to quit.

"Why?"

"Now that is a dumb question."

He begged to differ. He liked to smoke. It was a relaxation he needed after working all day.

"After? You smoke at the office, too."

Her tone was accusing. She spoke with the moral authority of one who has kicked the habit. Edward resisted, of course. Nothing had been proved against smoking; all the evidence was statistical. Besides, his father had smoked two packs a day and he was still going strong at eighty.

"With emphysema. Anyway, he quit smoking."

"I'll quit when I'm his age."

It took half a year for her campaign to take effect. When he did quit, Edward echoed her praises for the tobacco-free life. There were times when Vera felt she had won too much in persuading him. Had she secretly hoped he would tell her to go to hell and leave him alone? When he bought the pipe, she told herself she would say nothing if he began to smoke it, but he never even bought tobacco.

"My God, what a nag you are," Dolores said. "Get him well insured, and let him smoke and drink all he wants."

"He wanted to quit."

"Vera, nobody wants to quit smoking."

"Well, I couldn't make him do it if he didn't want to."

Dolores just looked at her. Maybe Edward would lapse. Maybe she would feign backsliding herself and give him an excuse. But she had honestly lost all desire to smoke. Watching Dolores and Howard lighting cigarette after cigarette, Vera had difficulty imagining herself doing the same. Yet she had, for years. She decided that Edward was as free of the memory as she was herself and stopped thinking about it.

And then one day Andrea surprised her by lighting a cigarette and exhaling a vast, shapeless cloud of smoke.

"That could be dangerous to your health. And mine."

"But you smoke." Andrea was faintly reminiscent of Joan Crawford in an old black and white movie, of the vintage where the air was always thick with cigarette smoke. Like the early *I Love Lucy* episodes.

"I used to smoke."

Andrea's green eyes lifted from her cigarette. "You've quit?"

"Yes."

"Why?"

"Why? I just did."

"Are you expecting?"

Even from an old friend, that was a terribly direct question. But Vera had no defense against it. Making light of it was impossible. She felt a sudden relief at being able to talk about it.

"I wish I were. Oh, God, how I wish I were."

"Is something wrong?"

"I don't know." Her voice caught, her lip trembled, tears formed in her eyes. She must not cry, not in front of Andrea, she mustn't. But she did. They were sitting in the sunroom. Andrea came to perch beside her on the couch, and Vera told her everything, including why she had quit smoking.

"Have you consulted with doctors?"

"Oh, yes. There's no reason for it. It just doesn't happen. Now that you know, you can say some prayers for us."

"I always do."

"Specific prayers. Say a novena. Do people still say novenas?"

Andrea just patted her hand. "I will say a novena."

But she seemed almost embarrassed by her promise. Imagine a nun uneasy at the mention of a novena, nine days of prayer for a special intention. Hadn't nuns invented the notion of a novena? Andrea did not know.

"Nuns have changed, Vera, as you may have noticed."

It was a day of confidences. Having made herself vulnerable with her tearful confession, Vera became an apt receiver of Andrea's story about her friend Alma, who had left her order and was now staying at Andrea's apartment in Oak Park.

"Temporarily?"

"She has a boyfriend."

"Isn't that why she left?"

Andrea's laugh restored their earlier mood, and soon Vera was hearing of one nun after another who had gone over the wall, how and why and all the peculiar twists of leaving. She heard about Sister Jeanne and her elopement with a married man. Another nun had gone on retreat in California to find she was housed with male as well as female religious. It was a coed retreat, aimed at helping them get in touch with themselves.

They got in touch with one another, too. Andrea's friend had fallen in love with a Christian Brother.

"The ones who make brandy?"

"I guess."

There were other tales, but suddenly Andrea stopped.

"I shouldn't be telling you these things."

"I shouldn't have told you I'm unable to get pregnant. That was personal."

Andrea lit another cigarette, and Vera said nothing. "I've thought of leaving myself, Vera. How could I not?"

"When will you go back?"

"Back?"

"To Green Bay."

"Vera, that's the point. It isn't there anymore. The orders we entered have ceased to exist."

Andrea had always spoken of the changes in the religious life in positive tones, as progress, as renewal, as having welcome effects. On this occasion she spoke with the sadness of someone whose youthful dreams had been stolen from her.

Is that why you had your teeth straightened?

That was the question Vera did not ask her old friend. But why would a nun be so vain of her appearance, particularly when the correction had been minimal?

From that day Vera no longer thought of Andrea as someone who would live out her life as a nun. Learning that there was no convent for Andrea to return to, Vera saw that her friend must inevitably recognize that her vocation had ceased to exist. Andrea Bauer had become a bachelor girl, and the time must come when she would meet a man who made her leaving final.

And whenever Andrea came onto the deck of the *Dental Flaws*, anchored in Belmont Harbor, wearing her own swimsuit, somewhat more modest than the one she had borrowed on her first visit, Vera could not ignore the effect of that scarcely concealed body on Edward.

5.

Andrea, after a dinner or two with the Thornes, preferred to see Vera downtown or in a campus coffee shop. The confidence in the sunroom was thus unusual in several ways. It was the first time she had really seen beneath the surface of Vera's and Edward's life. Of course she had wondered about the absence of children, but she had more or less assumed that they were just putting it off. After all, Vera was a successful lawyer, and Edward seemed more interested in hobbies and gadgets. Particularly his boat.

"What do you do with it in the winter?"

"Dry dock. We put it in the water again last weekend."

It was May of her second year in Chicago, and she had become Edward's dental patient. Sun fell in bars across his office, suggesting both imprisonment and freedom. Edward said he would be working on the boat that Wednesday. When he invited her to Belmont Harbor, it simply did not occur to her that Vera would not be there.

"Lawyers work every day," Edward said, handing

her down into the dinghy. He had already tossed in her tote bag, which contained her new swimsuit.

The sky was overcast, threatening rain, but Edward assured her that did not matter. He maneuvered among the other anchored boats. They all looked alike. No wonder owners gave them such outrageous names. *Dental Flaws!*

"Who thought of that, you?"

"Vera." When he grinned, his long, lean face, which in repose had a kind of solemn look, came alive. His teeth were not exactly an ad for his profession, too large, too much gum showing when he smiled, a pivot tooth he would not have tolerated in a patient. "My best suggestion was *Naval Drill.*"

"That's good!"

"Dental Flaws is better."

But Andrea thought it a question of which was worse. Being alone with him in the little rowboat was different from having coffee with him in his office. Andrea would not have admitted that she was using those chats to pry into his life with Vera. Vera's husband. That is what Edward was to her; he existed on the edge of Vera's reality. Did anyone see him otherwise?

"Don't you ever see other dentists?"

"Socially? No . . . I guess we don't."

Everyone he mentioned had been Vera's friend first. Including herself. Andrea felt the first dangerous surge of pity for Edward.

Having coffee in his office, talking aimlessly, was somehow faintly exciting, as if Andrea were illicitly tapping into Vera's marriage. She neither expected nor wanted Edward to confide in her or tell her things he shouldn't, and he didn't; nonetheless, she realized that she wanted to discover Edward's perspective on his marriage. And he was curious about her as well, if only as Vera's friend.

"I can't imagine either one of you as girls."

"How do you mean?"

He didn't know exactly, but he enjoyed hearing about the things she and Vera had done when they were younger.

"When did you go into the convent?"

"Not until after high school."

"Right after high school?" He looked shocked. Andrea supposed it did seem very young to be making so serious a decision. There were many who would agree with him, and indeed, many who had entered young had been among the first to leave once the council made it easier to do. But the nuns who remained had also entered young.

"How long were you in?"

"How long? You mean in the novitiate or what?"

"The convent."

It dawned on Andrea then that he did not realize she was still a nun. She tried to explain that being in the convent was no longer simply a matter of physical location, it was a state of mind.

"It's all in your mind?" His smile was skeptical.

"What could be more important?" Andrea went on a bit about the primacy of mind; it was, after all, what made a person a person, and it was intention, wasn't it, that made an action the kind of action it was? Tapping a stick could be nervousness, sending a message, testing for a concealed trap, establishing rhythm for a dance.

"Stop, please. What did you study in school?"

"Philosophy. Just like Vera."

Her next appointment with him was late in the day, and they went out for a drink afterward, to a terribly crowded bar. Edward's reaction when she lit a cigarette was almost conspiratorial.

"I didn't know you smoked."

"I'm not proud of it. Vera told me you used to smoke."

He had taken one from her package and was rolling it between thumb and forefinger. He tried it in the vee of his fingers.

She said, "Light it."

He shrugged but avoided her eyes. She pressed her lighter and held the flame toward him. He inhaled deeply as he lit the cigarette.

"Don't tell Vera," he whispered, the words gusting forth on exhaled smoke.

She found that the oddest request. Was he afraid of Vera? Of course, to smoke after having quit was an admission of weakness, and naturally he would not want to tell her he had weakened.

"I feel like a temptress."

Having lit one cigarette, he chain-smoked there in the bar, drinking three Scotch and waters in forty-five minutes. He seemed unaffected by the alcohol and exhilarated by the cigarettes—he bought a package in the bar before they left—and Andrea did not feel unsafe on the drive to Oak Park. At the curb in front of her building, he leaned toward her and kissed her cheek, and she hopped out and ran toward the door trying to pretend she was not blushing and smiling idiotically.

"Who was that?" Alma asked, twisting on the couch to look over her shoulder. She wore a housecoat, her hair was in curlers, the television was on, as it doubtless had been all day. The glass of Coke beside her was full. She must have looked out the window when she got up to get a drink.

"My dentist."

Alma gave her an arch look.

"Who is the husband of my oldest friend. What have you done all day?"

Nothing. Meaning that she had slept until noon and then curled up in front of the television. Alma had adopted a vegetable existence. Scolding her only brought tears. Making suggestions got an irritated reaction. Andrea was beginning to wonder how wise she had been to offer Alma open-ended hospitality.

"Any calls?"

"For me? One."

It was in response to the ad Andrea had persuaded Alma to place in *The Chicago Catholic*. A man named Rupert, pastor of a parish in a western suburb. Alma would meet him for an interview the following day.

Did either of them have a premonition then, with the television murmuring inanities in a corner of the room, that Alma would be going to meet her destiny on the morrow? Andrea felt only relief, hoping the end of the extended visit was in sight. Alma, perhaps sensing the same thing, was almost petulant.

Chuck Rupert was thirty-nine, with thick, wavy blond hair. He had a doctorate from Louvain and had taught at a college that was now defunct. He was associate pastor of Mother of God and engaged in putting together a parish team that would implement the reforms of Vatican II as he understood them: a parish council, adult education classes, liturgical innovations. Alma's background was a plus; she was offered the job— and refused.

"You refused!"

"Andrea, I did not leave the convent in order to become a church mouse."

"But what in the name of God do you want to do?"

"I don't know!" Alma's voice was shrill; tears would soon follow, perhaps hysteria. She was frightened, and Andrea's heart went out to her. She sat beside Alma and took her in her arms.

"Look, Alma, think of this as temporary, something to do until something you really want turns up."

"He wants someone permanent."

Andrea talked to Rupert, explaining the situation. He sounded dubious. He needed someone to rely on, not a reluctant weakling.

"Give her a chance?"

"Does she want it?"

It would have seemed absurd then to imagine that within four months Chuck Rupert and Alma would be married. But when Alma told her, Andrea was not surprised. There had been too many indications. Chuck seemed forever in the apartment when she got home. There was at least one weekend that Alma was very vague about. Andrea was not condemnatory. How could she have been? By then she herself was in well over her head with the husband of her oldest friend.

His firm hand on her bottom boosted her aboard. The rain had begun to fall before they reached the *Dental Flaws*. Edward scrambled up after her and had trouble with the padlock on the cabin door. When the lock finally sprang and he rolled up the door, Andrea scooted into the darkness with relief. In a matter of minutes her hair had become drenched. Her blouse was plastered to her skin, and her slacks were almost as wet.

Edward flicked on the cabin light, pulled a towel from a locker, and pointed at the head. She wrapped the towel around her hair and got her swimsuit out of her bag. It was the only change she had.

When she came out, she felt as if she were modeling for him. He had turned on the radio and the heat. The plastic cup he held was full of coffee. They shared it. She was very conscious that she was wearing only a swimsuit, that she was alone with Edward in a very small space, that the rain was coming down heavily all around them.

"Is this called a hold?"

"No. This is." He put his arms around her and pulled her against him. His clothes were wet from the rain. She pressed her forehead against his chest, wondering what she should do now. She did not feel shock. She did not feel disgust. Was this how he held Vera? She lifted her face to his surprisingly gentle kiss.

When she got free of him, she said, "You're wet."

He nodded and began to unbutton his shirt. Andrea was mesmerized by what was happening. What would he do next? He took her into his arms, and this time she closed her eyes and pressed her lips against his bare chest. She kept her eyes closed until they were together in the narrow bunk and things she had wondered about since she was a girl became much simpler than she would have believed.

Afterward, cradled in his arms, sharing a cigarette, she was filled with thoughts of Vera. Was Edward thinking of Vera, too? It seemed wiser to concentrate on the sound of raindrops and succumb to the lulling rhythm of the rocking boat.

6.

"I thought you had a roommate."

"She got married."

"Married? Wasn't she a nun?"

"She left."

Edward nodded, his eyes going out of focus.

"She married a priest."

"God."

"It's not the first time that's happened, Edward. Don't you read the newspaper?"

"As little as possible."

"How do you get the news, television?"

"I don't. Who needs to be depressed? When I'm not at the office, I play racquet ball, I jog, I sail, I get on the radio."

"Whom do you talk to?"

He shrugged. "People like myself."

"Dentists?"

"Not many. Foreign dentists don't have much of an income."

"Are all hams rich?"

"I wouldn't say rich."

"So what do you talk about? Do you talk politics?"

"Hell no."

"The weather?"

"We talk about all kinds of things."

"It sounds like a great big party line. But I can't imagine what the gossip is about."

Was Edward really as simple as he seemed? Andrea was certain there had to be more to him than he revealed in conversation. But maybe there wasn't. Maybe that was his appeal. He was certainly a relief after the cerebral types she had been spending her time with.

That Wednesday on the boat, they had spent hours together in a cramped cabin, penned in by the rain, not saying much, just being close. They had the thermos of coffee Edward had brought, as well as a package of Oreo cookies. If that first time had not been so prolonged, it would have been easier to treat it as a lapse. But she had given Edward a claim on her, something she did not at first regret. Not that she wanted to meet him again at Belmont Harbor. "Your place?" he had asked, and since Alma was now gone, Andrea had agreed.

"How old was the priest?" Edward asked.

"The priest? Oh, you mean the one Alma married? I don't know. Forty?"

"Older than her."

"Yes."

"What brought it on?"

"Loneliness, I suppose. What brought it on with you?"

"You mean with Vera?"

"Who else?"

She had never fished, but Andrea imagined it felt like this. Except in this case the fisher felt as endangered as her prey.

"Vera thought it was only your second time aboard." The previous weekend the three of them had gone sailing. It was late July. Her affair with Edward had been going on for months.

"Would you have wanted me to tell her differently?"

"What impressed me was your calmness."

"Oh?"

"You could have been an actress."

"Maybe I have been."

"You never acted like a nun."

"What do you mean?"

"I never thought you were a nun."

"That's like saying I didn't think you were a dentist. And I didn't. I thought of you as Vera's husband. As you are. Which makes me think of myself as . . . What should I think of myself as, Edward?"

"My wife."

"You already have a wife."

"If you stop being a nun, I can stop being a husband."

"Making us both traitors?"

"Is that how you think of it?"

"I try to think of it as little as possible."

The following Wednesday they spent on the boat, a

great improvement over her apartment in Oak Park, the breeze off the lake sufficient for them to welcome the sun.

"Should we be on deck like this?"

"Why not?"

"Someone will see us. Someone will ask you who the woman was."

"And I will say a friend of my wife."

" 'A friend of my wife.' "

"Who is going to be my wife."

"Don't say that, Edward. You have no intention of leaving Vera. I don't want you to leave Vera."

"Okay."

"I think I should go."

"We just got here."

"Edward, what is the point? You've had your little triumph."

"You mean I led you astray?"

"I take my share of the blame."

"Let's go below."

"Just like that?"

"I'll carry you."

"Edward! For heaven's sake, put me down."

"If you're good, I'll show you my dinghy."

Edward acquainted her with passion, with a whole world of delightful adolescent nastiness she had never known, with the pleasant ache of treachery, with love.

Their relationship would have been psychologically intolerable if she had not come to see she loved him. She had always found him attractive, someone she could be at ease with. She had thought this was be-

cause he was Vera's husband, and thus already a kind
of friend, but it was more than that. He was tall and
good looking in a way not easy to describe, and he had
a vulnerable, crooked smile Andrea found difficult to
resist. And why should she resist the affection she felt
for Vera's husband? It was a natural extension of their
friendship.

She had betrayed that friendship many times now.
The treachery came easily, as if she had been readying
herself for years to destroy every link to girlhood inno-
cence. That she, a nun, should feel more worldly-wise
than Vera was the ultimate irony. But Andrea had
never dreamed that Edward would have the courage to
speak of them to his wife.

7.

Her pressed jeans were stuffed into ankle-high
suede boots, her very full woolly sweater enveloped
her in pink, and her hair, cut short, brushed back on
the sides, was still parted in the middle. She held an
unlit filter-tipped cigarette as she leaned sincerely toward Vera.

"Say whatever you want to. I deserve it."

"Are you still a nun?"

A little smile as she sat back. "Is that all that inter-
ests you?"

"Edward has the impression the two of you are going
to marry."

Andrea lit the cigarette. Was it a matter of practice, inhaling, holding it as she studied the ceiling, then letting the smoke go in a cloud? Vera could imagine Andrea doing it in front of a mirror. She could imagine Andrea doing anything but making love to Edward.

"He says you have been to bed together."

"If you can call those things on the boat beds."

On the boat. Andrea a vision in a borrowed swimsuit. Had she invited a viper into her nest? All those memories of nights aboard with Edward would have to be expunged.

"Did you go sailing together?"

"No. Vera, you don't want all the sordid details."

"Sordid? You should be telling me how wonderful it all was. I expect you to tell me that God wanted you to sleep with Edward."

"Vera, please."

"That is what Edward says."

Andrea chose not to talk about it, and Vera could believe that Edward, untutored by Andrea, had come up with the divine command excuse for his infidelity. Andrea's reaction suggested how foreign such talk had become to her.

"*Are* you still a nun?"

"I sent in my resignation."

"When?"

"Does it matter?"

"Was it because of Edward?"

"Do you really want to know?"

"Of course I want to know. I've been your confidante from the beginning, haven't I? Remember how we talked about it when we were in high school? And after you went away, we wrote about it. Andrea, do you remember when you came home in your habit for your father's funeral?"

Putting out the cigarette was also dramatic. Andrea studied the ashes she had created as if they were a reminder of mortality. "That was a long time ago."

"What happened?"

"It's a long story. Vera, look at me. Do I look the least bit like the girl in the habit?"

"You always defended dressing like other women."

"I don't mean the way I *dress*. Vera, I didn't leave the convent. It left me. After I got my master's, what choice did I have? I couldn't go back to Green Bay. There wasn't a community there to go back to, not really. My superior as much as told me I was on my own. Learn a trade, support yourself. Not in those words, of course, but that was the message. So I came to Chicago."

"You made it sound like your decision."

"Oh, it was, in a way. The point is, I had no choice. Vera, there aren't any convents or nuns or peace or quiet anymore."

"No one kneeling in chapel saying prayers for the rest of us?"

"No."

"Do you still pray, Andrea?"

"I guess I deserve that."

"I don't mean to taunt you. I am genuinely curious. You're the only one I ever heard speak of prayer as if it were truly important."

"That, too, was a long time ago."

Andrea lit another cigarette, less stylishly now, but

she might have been setting fire to their youth, their friendship, all her dreams of sanctity.

"I want you to keep away from Edward."

"Believe me, if I could have spared you pain . . ."

"Do you love him?"

"You know the answer to that."

"Tell me."

"Vera, your quarrel is not with me. It's with Edward. Obviously Edward felt the need for something he did not have."

"Adultery?"

"I am not going to argue with you."

"Aren't you ashamed?"

"Yes. I've been ashamed of myself for years."

"Have there been others?"

"Vera, that is cruel." Andrea got up from her sofa. "Let's not talk about it anymore. Not now. I am sorry you have been hurt. Blame me if you like. But you might ask yourself whether anything you did—or didn't do—enters into what happened."

As girls they had had fallings out, but never a physical fight, pulling hair, scratching; only cruel words, periods of estrangement, silence. Thus there was no precedent for what Vera did when Andrea pulled the door open and stood by it, avoiding Vera's eyes.

Vera strode up to Andrea and slapped her in the face, as hard as she could, swinging her arm in a great looping arc. Losing her balance Andrea stumbled backward, tripped over the coffee table, and crashed onto the floor between it and the sofa.

Vera went through the door without waiting to see if Andrea was hurt.

PART FIVE

Get Thee to a Nunnery

I .

The man at the front desk in the Hotel Columbus in Rome called her room to say that a Mr. Kenneth Stewart wished to see her. "Stewart?"

The clerk, who was inordinately but not unjustly proud of the English he had perfected during a year in Newark, thought she was correcting his pronunciation. "S-t-e-w-a-r-t," he said coldly. He even pronounced the alphabet in English. There was the sound of another voice in the background. "He wishes to speak with you. Should I put him on?"

"Of course."

"Mrs. Thorne, this is Ken. We met—"

"Of course. I don't think I knew your family name."

"Are you busy?"

Busy? She had been staring down into the courtyard, which was wet with rain, and beyond its walls to a church on the Borgo Santo Spirito whose facade and white marble steps looked like a water color. Her content had been animal, totally devoid of thought. To live alone like this in Rome forever seemed something she could easily do. It would be like a convent cell, with church bells quartering every hour.

"I'd like to talk with you."

"Give me a few minutes. Tell the clerk to show you the bar. It doesn't look at all like a bar."

It looked like a Renaissance salon, frescoed walls, islands of furniture, which was of two kinds, stiff and uncomfortable, and plush and too comfortable. The floor lamps wore shades that seemed to antedate the invention of electricity. The bar was an isolated wooden structure angling one corner, ten feet long, five feet high, with four very high stools set before it. Ken stood in the middle of the room.

"This is a cozy little place."

"The guest rooms really are cozy. Come, I'll show you around."

The dining room drew appreciative murmurs, but he agreed that the breakfast room was even nicer. That is, the view was nicer. Two rows of tables in a long room with a dark red tile floor. Vera touched the first table on a corner, and it tipped obligingly.

"They all do. Every morning, after you sit, the waiter wads a napkin under one of the legs to steady the table. It is important to pretend that the problem has just arisen for the first time."

The view was of the courtyard she had been contemplating from the window of her room. A fountain almost as large as those in the Piazza San Pietro dominated the area. The vines on the wall, the wisteria, even the slate gray of the pavement, took on richer colors from the rain.

"The Knights of the Holy Sepulcher," Ken said, picking up a plate and studying the Maltese cross. He knew quite a lot about the Hotel Columbus, as Vera observed. His smile was fleeting and disarming.

152

"I looked it up before coming. I wanted to impress you."

She gave him a little smile in return. "Let's go back to the bar. Would you like tea?"

He had left his umbrella at the desk, and that had been his only protection against the rain. The bottoms of his pants were wet, and the sleeves of his tweed jacket looked damp. Vera was glad he agreed to tea rather than asking for something cold.

"Why did you want to impress me?"

He returned his cup to its saucer. "I sensed the other day that you did not trust me. No doubt because I am a seminarian. It was obvious you wondered how I had become a friend of Katy's."

"That question did occur to me."

"I am breaking no rules, Mrs. Thorne."

"I was worried about hearts."

"Katy?" He laughed. "As far as she's concerned, we're just pals."

"And as far as you're concerned?"

"That's the problem."

He was not forbidden to see girls in general or Katy in particular; he was almost urged to.

"There have been so many who have left the priesthood. I guess the theory is that they had no notion of alternatives. So, if we do and still become priests, the chances are we will stick with it."

"That's the theory?"

"What do you think of it?"

"Not much. Should engaged people date others to test their love? It's an odd view of life. You try everything first and then you choose one thing seriously. But

153

who can try everything? I don't think choosing is like that."

"I gather your divorce was not your idea?"

The question was impertinent, but his manner was so ingenuous that she was not offended. Or was he practicing being a confessor? His hair, randomly arranged, was oddly reminiscent of Katy's. His eyes were of a blue so pale they seemed translucent.

She said, "How do you feel toward Katy?"

"Like leaving the seminary."

"In order to be with her?"

He thought about that. "I'm not sure. She's not the first girl I've gone with. In high school I went steady."

"Is it still called that?"

"It is in Mankato."

"So what's the problem?"

"Katy makes me wonder if I want to be a priest."

"But if you turn from the priesthood, it won't be toward Katy?"

"I don't know. We're both young."

He had put a slice of lemon into his cup after filling it with tea and was now submerging it with spoonsful of sugar. What did he expect from her? What she had withheld the other day, not realizing she was: her approval. He needed her endorsement of his relationship, whatever it was, with Katy. He would need the approval of everyone he knew for whatever he did. Vera was suddenly certain that this was Kenneth Stewart's fate. He wished to live his personal life on the basis of a consensus. Of course, there would always be a minority view—as he now took hers to be—and then a dialogue would be necessary. If she did not ultimately form part of the consensus, he could accept her dissent, since he would have shown flexibility and openness by discussing the matter with her.

"I am sure you'll do the right thing, Ken."

"But what do you think the right thing is?"

"For you?"

"For me and Katy."

The pale blue eyes were receptive. He wanted her input, he really did.

She had thought of Andrea the other day while having dinner with Katy and Ken, but Andrea had not doubted her vocation until after she came to Chicago. As a young girl, once she had set her face in the direction of the convent, she had not wavered. Vera had felt diminished by Andrea's certitude.

"Do you pray?" she asked Ken.

She had disturbed his poise, though that had not been her intention.

"The other night I told you about my childhood friend who became a nun. She was the first one who ever spoke to me of prayer. I have never forgotten what she said, it was so strange. Though I am sure she doesn't remember the conversation herself now. Do you pray?"

"The liturgy forms an important part of our day."

"The liturgy."

"The Mass. The Eucharist."

"But that's public. I mean private prayer, silent prayer."

"Meditation?"

"Yes."

"It is not emphasized as much as it used to be. I take that on the word of older priests. The fear now is that it can lead one to think of one's relation to God as merely private."

"As opposed to public?"

"Well, we speak of the people of God."

And the kingdom of God is within you. She did not say this aloud. She did not want to argue. She imagined that silent prayer must be a buffer against distraction, against losing oneself in external things, things said aloud, gestures performed. But to sit in silence and sink into the presence of God—was that self-indulgent?

"What did you think when your friend entered the convent?"

"I thought she was mad. It seemed like dying, a kind of dying. She spoke of it that way."

Ken was smiling indulgently at the image of Andrea that her words had conjured up for him. But Vera was far more impressed by the Andrea that was than by this contemporary version of the seminarian.

"Why did she leave?"

"It was gradual, I think. Doesn't it seem odd that we can surprise ourselves, come to see that we have already made a decision without quite realizing it? Andrea ceased to be a nun long before she knew it."

"Andrea."

"It's a nice name, isn't it?"

"It means manly. The Greek stem."

"How inappropriate."

"What is she doing now?"

The waiter who had brought their tea had exchanged

his white linen jacket for a red one and was fussing behind the bar. It was going on six o'clock.

"She is thinking of marrying."

"Do you know whom?"

For a moment she wondered if Katy had told him, but she was not sure how much Katy knew. It was impossible to tell what those pale blue eyes concealed.

"She is going to marry my husband."

2.

The church she saw across the courtyard from the Hotel Columbus would have been, anywhere else in the world, a cathedral, a basilica, the biggest church in town, but here in Rome it was just another huge church. Not that it was ignored. Whenever Vera stood at her window, there seemed to be a constant traffic in and out, and kids played noisily on the great half-circle steps, pockmarked, gray in ordinary daylight, white only when it rained. Yet twice she had gone to visit and found the doors closed. The second time she continued walking in the direction of Katy's residence and ended in the vastness of San Andrea del Valle.

The name caught her attention, of course. A woman and man had taken up their station just outside the door, surrounded by plastic bags filled with junk. They were sharing some bread and a bottle of wine; the woman did not have enough teeth to chew easily, the man had one blind eye and the look of an idiot, yet they sat there like lovers, sharing their food. Were they lovers?

The woman shifted her bread and put out a hand to Vera, a creased, leathery-smooth palm. Her companion put out a hand, too, less enthusiastically. Vera opened her purse and took out the first bill she touched. Ten thousand lire. Much too much, but little enough. The money was gathered in and disappeared in a moment, and Vera continued into the church, trying to repress the wave of righteousness that swept over her.

The interior was even barer than St. Peter's—no pews, no chairs, not even any wooden separaters, just a vast marble expanse leading to the distant altar. Vera had imagined kneeling or sitting, but she had the sense of long-distance communication as she stood and brought the far-off altar into focus, forming a prayer in her mind.

Our Father, who art in heaven . . . And was He here in this vastness of plaster and marble, high, fluted columns and massive statues, tons of gracefully draped cloth and light-as-lead angel wings? God is everywhere. Closing her eyes did not help. She opened them, looked at her joined hands, told herself that those hands, she herself, the whole world, would be instant nothingness if God did not sustain them. The thought did not help. It was too abstract. She wished she could form an image of Jesus, a particular human being, so high, so near or far, someone to talk and listen to. His eyes and hair would be of some definite color. But all she could come up with was the saccharine, wimpy Jesus of calendar art. Prayer had sounded easy until she tried it. Of course she could recite the words of the Lord's Prayer. And feel like Hamlet's uncle. "My words fly up, my thoughts remain below; words without thoughts, never to heaven go."

"What did you say to Ken?"
They sat on a couch with cracked plastic cushions in the lobby. Katy's question was not hostile, as Vera had expected. Her niece, in corduroy skirt and T-shirt emblazoned with the letters ND ("Notre Dame?" "No, North Dakota"), looked at her as if at a stranger. But then they *were* strangers, whatever the connection of blood.
"What did he say I said?"
"That Uncle Edward plans to marry a nun."
"I don't know why I told him that."
"Is it true?"
"Not completely. She has stopped being a nun."
Katy shook her head, but the story washed off her. "Ken was miffed that you wouldn't tell him more about it."
After her unintentional revelation, Vera had wanted to escape to her room. But she had succeeded for the first time in engaging the total attention of the young man from Mankato. He wanted to know her feelings about the matter. He wanted to know how close she and Andrea had been. His questions had an insinuating tone Vera did not like.
"But it is a classical case. She wants the man you had."
"That is classical?"

He slid to the edge of his cushion and opened his hands as if he were saying Mass. "Your husband is a substitute for you."

"That is ridiculous. How can you make up theories about someone you've never met?"

"It is because I don't know her that I can see more clearly. Was she jealous of you when you were young?"

It was difficult not to laugh. Andrea jealous of her? It was the other way around, if anything.

"Maybe it was mutual," he conceded. How assured he was. Human beings dropped into prepared categories; complicated actions became the satisfying fulfillment of a theory.

"You and Andrea would get along. She has become a counselor."

He did not find this strange. He himself was getting psychological counseling as a part of his seminary training. From a priest. He called him Gerry, but Gerry was a priest. He lived alone in Rome; Ken went to his apartment beyond the Forum for weekly sessions.

"He has helped me a lot."

"What was the problem?"

He looked at her for a moment. "It's why I can empathize with you and your friend. It is also why she frightens me a bit. Most people outgrow it; it is simply a youthful thing. But for her to do what she is doing at her age, well . . ."

Vera did not understand. He had no objection at all to being more explicit. They had finally found the topic he preferred, his psyche, his orientation, sexual. Was he gay? That was the question he was putting to himself under Gerry's tutelage. Going with Katy fitted into this exploration of himself.

He seemed to change physically as he talked, though of course he did not. The pale blue eyes seemed feline, the hands too graceful. And was there the suggestion of a lisp as he spoke of Gerry and their lengthy sessions? Vera was appalled. Ken had represented the heterosexual predator, menacing her niece from behind a religious mask. What had he become? This setting became him, tea in a Renaissance room, whispers under the frescoes, an older woman's ear into which to pour his psychic story.

She said to Katy, "He wanted to tell me all about myself. I did more listening than talking."

"I know the feeling."

"How much has he told you?"

"You mean wondering if he's gay?"

Vera gave up. What was happening to the world? Youngsters spoke of dark and arcane matters as if they knew everything. Theoretically? How? Dear God, she did not want to know. Ignorance exerted an almost sensuous attraction.

"I'm going to Innsbruck," Katy said.

To ski. With four girl friends. Without Ken. Ken seemed no longer the factor he had been when Vera first arrived. Could she report to Dolores that the crisis was over?

"I don't know why she was worried in the first place."

"Maybe because you burst into tears on the phone."

"That was dumb," Katy conceded.

161

"Have you called home lately?"

She hadn't. They decided to put through a call together; Vera would pay for it. With the six-hour difference, it was midmorning in Chicago. Vera stood at a discreet distance while Katy talked with her mother. The grandmotherly woman checking the mail behind the desk was a nun, in charge of the Rome program. She wore an open coat sweater, a dress so nondescript it might have been a habit; her hair was a mass of snarls. Her name was Monica. Vera had been introduced to her three times, and each time as if for the first. She looked at Vera with a half-bewildered half smile.

"Can I help you?"

"I'm waiting for Katy. My niece."

"Oh, yes." Sister Monica seemed to be trying unsuccessfully to remember something. Perhaps what it had once been like to be a nun.

"Well, she certainly sounds all right," Dolores said when Vera got on the phone.

"I think you're right."

"Everything settled?"

Katy, three feet away, her weight on one sneaker, looked sardonically at her aunt. "I would say so. Did Katy tell you about Austria?"

Katy went into a wild pantomime, shaking her head, erasing the remark with her hands, looking at her aunt with unconcealed dismay.

"Austria?" Dolores asked.

"It will be in the paper tonight," Vera said. "I'm leaving Rome."

"For Austria?"

"Paris."

With that answer she made up her mind. She would go north to Paris and then home. It was as if she had accomplished her mission. On the slopes of Innsbruck, Katy would forget the seminarian of undetermined sexual orientation, and back home in Chicago her mother could relax.

3.

In Paris, on the rue de Bac, she came upon the chapel in which the Blessed Virgin Mary had appeared to Catherine Laboure.

By accident. It was a Sunday afternoon, and she had decided to take the train to Lisieux, but when she arrived at the Gare St.-Lazare, there seemed to be no way to get there and back that day. Return to her hotel and pack a few things? By then it would be so late that by the time she arrived in the town of the Little Flower, Sainte Thérèse, she would have to wait until morning to see anything.

So she got back on the Metro and, when it reached the rue de Bac, got off on impulse. Something had happened here, and she could not remember what. She came up into an intersection, the streets full of fallen sycamore leaves, tan and gold, a Sunday afternoon emptiness. The rue de Bac went in two directions, and Vera chose one at random.

She came upon a little park in which a bust of Chateaubriand stood on a plinth. The bust looked across the street toward a house identified as the place where Chateaubriand had died. Chateaubriand? Steak. She would have to look him up. The little park with its wrought iron fence, the plaque on the house commemorating the man's death, the Sunday afternoon peace of Paris, piqued her curiosity. But it was not this that explained the vague familiarity of the rue de Bac.

Farther along there was a gray facade with a statue of the Blessed Virgin high above an arched entrance leading to an inner courtyard. Vera went in. To her right a house, a gate, and straight ahead a little church. It was a seminary, the foreign mission seminary, and inside she found the tomb of Saint Theophane Venard and a painting depicting his martyrdom in what came to be Vietnam. He and the Little Flower had been pen pals! Suddenly Vera felt in the grips of a planned afternoon, as if the little Carmelite saint were guiding her steps.

At the *recueil* she asked what else there was on the rue de Bac. The woman, Asian, did not understand her English. But she stood and pointed. Then she wrote a number on a sheet of paper and gave it to Vera. 180 rue de Bac.

The facade was exactly like that of the foreign mission seminary, the statue of the Virgin identical, but when Vera went through the gate, she found herself in a crowd. The gate opened onto a narrow courtyard, which led between a wall of bas-reliefs on one side and storefronts on the other to the entrance of a church. Mass intentions were accepted; there were restrooms for pilgrims, "Hommes" and "Dames," a store where one could buy miraculous medals. There were even little

vending machines filled with medals. It was the miraculous medals and the great comic strip of a wall that
told Vera where she had come.

The chapel was full, every seat taken. Along the back
wall were benches, and eventually Vera took advantage
of a departure and sat. All around her people said their
prayers, rosaries for the most part. Next to Vera was a
woman, perhaps sixty, a striking profile, her dress *très
chic*, whose gloved hands gripped her purse. Her eyes
were shut. Her lips did not move. She might have been
asleep, but she was not. Vera, almost blinded by the
brightness of the altar, a mass of candles reinforced
with electric lights, stole glances at the praying woman,
and a thought formed in her mind. If she can do it, I
can.

She shut her eyes, and the afterimage of that too
bright altar slowly faded into darkness. The bustling
sounds around her also faded, and Vera abandoned herself to the conviction that she had been led here, that it
had not been mere chance that prompted her to leave
the Metro when she did, to walk in the direction she
had. She felt enveloped in a benevolent presence. She
did not say or think a word.

She thought of it later as the first time she prayed.
When she was interrupted, it was by the beginning of
a Mass. That morning she had heard Mass at Saint-
Séverin, but she remained for this one. When she left,
she resolved to return the following day. Once lucky,
twice charmed. That chapel was a place where she could
pray as she had dreamed of doing.

Paris.

She had been to Paris once before, with Edward, four

days of hectic, expensive fun, dinner at Le Doyen, drinking too much and listening to violins in a Hungarian bar until four in the morning. They had looked into Notre Dame, they had sat across from Saint-Germain-des-Prés, having drinks at the Deux Magots. What had it meant, that swift trip? Diversion. Fun. Why not? They had never taken the Metro. Would it have mattered if they had?

Going down into a subway station was like a descent into purgatory at least. It was not that Vera felt unsafe or threatened on the trains, or even waiting for them, although once a drunk had come weaving along the platform, enraged, shouting against the world. His eyes would not focus. People moved back against the curved yellow wall to let him pass. How easily he could have fallen from the platform and been killed. Would his eventual death be any different? He would plunge drunkenly into the justice or mercy of eternity. The thought did not make Vera feel superior to him. Or to any of the derelicts who seemed to haunt the Metro, sleeping on the uncomfortable plastic seats or, oh, luxury, claiming the tiled ledge behind them.

France had reached out into the world, into Africa, into the Orient, and now the colonies colonized France. Blacks, Asians, Arabs, aliens from everywhere seemed to have taken over Paris. What wild hopes had brought them to the City of Light? And now they hurtled along in this underground tunnel, on the way to menial jobs, or, defeated, flooded their blood with alcohol and slept on ledges in the subway. What exotic dreams awaited them in drunken sleep—jungles, desert landscapes, islands, blue sky and sun and self-respect?

Riding the Metro was like reading Dante, and Vera felt ridiculously self-absorbed when she studied the blank faces in the car, black and yellow and brown and mixtures of them all, men and women who combined in their persons races that had been unaware of one another only a few generations ago. Mongrels, hybrids, but who is not?

Her troubles with Edward seemed a mild joke; remembered conversations with Andrea about self-fulfillment, self-discovery, were revealed for what they were—egocentric vanity. Vera recalled her grievances with Edward—she had been irked when he listened to her with half an ear, when he wanted to stay home on nights she would have liked to go out and vice versa. Out of such trivia she had built a case against him time and time again. Why had he not been nicer to her? Their life together—before Andrea—now seemed a time of impossible ease and comfort. Could any of her companions on the Metro imagine the luxury she had taken for granted? If they noticed Americans or other tourists at all, it could only be with incomprehension. They were as incomprehensible to Vera.

Could one look at such people, products of who knew what fugitive mating, as meant for an eternal destiny? Even Dante had concentrated on notables, as if prominence in this world made their eternal destiny more important.

When she returned to the rue de Bac the following day, the chapel was less crowded, and Vera was able to go forward and see the effigy of a nun beneath a side altar. At first she thought it was a real cadaver. Of course it could not be. But in the moment before the realization came, the peace, the permanence of that effigy, seemed the promise of the life the woman had led, the life whose symbol was the religious habit she wore.

For the first time Vera let the thought form itself in her mind.

I want to be a nun.

Dear God, let me be a nun.

4.

She changed planes at Dulles, went through customs there, and thus did not disembark in the international terminal at O'Hare. She was spared the sight of all those joyous reunions, the intrepid explorers back from their adventures in darkest Europe.

But if Vera smiled, it was at herself. It was she who hurried through the terminal, weaving her way among salesmen and athletes and random travelers, perhaps a professor or two, a bureaucrat come from Washington to check up on his provincial colleagues, grieving relatives on their way to or from death. Thousands of lives, as many scales on which to measure importance, and she was returned with the dream of living the rest of her life in the presence of God.

As if that were a place. As if she had a choice.

Throughout the long, once-interrupted flight, she had thought of her new ambition. It was like wanting to take up ballet at thirty-seven, or to begin voice lessons. The feeling that had swept over her in the chapel on the rue de Bac was the whim of a tourist, something possible only in another land, out of her own context. When she was home, common sense would return.

It was that, the return of common sense, that she expected as she swung through the terminal, feeling the small medal she had bought on the rue de Bac a slightly uncomfortable presence on her upper chest.

In Washington she might have telephoned Dolores, but she decided against it. She wanted to slip back into her normal life without fanfare, without greeting. She would take a taxi to her apartment.

The apartment showed no evidence of her three-week absence, but then she had made little imprint on the place since moving in, embarked on a new life alone. The familiar strangeness was not unwelcome now; almost it seemed another hotel room on her journey away from what she had been and toward . . .

In the living room she turned slowly until her eyes met her reflection in the mirror over the couch. The mirror was a relic from her home in Evanston, and it was the past that looked out of it at her, a past whose loss she had lamented before her impulsive trip to Europe. She did not like the self she saw: successful, self-possessed, attractive, abandoned and thus full of self-pity. Could she honestly say she missed Edward?

It had seemed important to her sense of betrayal to think that her love for Edward persisted, however fickle he had proved to be. The truth was, she had difficulty forming a distinct image of him in her mind. There was, of course, no photograph of him in the apartment. Did memories of pleasure assail her? She found that when clinically recalled, such almost mythic moments as their Cana weekend had lost their potency. Those nights aboard the *Dental Flaws?* It had been the night and the stars and the peaceful movement of the water she had loved. Add or subtract Edward, it would have been the same. Yes, she could have lived without Edward. What made the difference was that he had betrayed her with Andrea.

Before leaving for Europe, Vera had agreed to another meeting with Andrea. The Palmer House? Andrea agreed, apparently not seeing the irony.

"Vera, I thought everything was over between you and Edward."

"Did he tell you that?" Her eyes widened, then fell. Deceived by her lover?

"I'm sorry."

But for what? Andrea had so many things to feel sorry for.

"Vera, I will go away. He'll come back to you."

"When everything is over between us?"

"Obviously it isn't."

Vera closed her eyes on the pain. Andrea had become an expert on her life with Edward.

"Take him back. I'll go."

"Andrea, if you say that once more, I will scratch your eyes out."

She had hated Andrea. For Edward she could feel, or feign to feel, indifference, but she hated Andrea so deeply it made her sick to the stomach. The mirror now showed only a travel-weary woman who was different from the one whose image she had seen in it before her trip. Rising young lawyer? Collector of royalties on a software program for law firms? Childless but adjusted wife? No label fit. Aspiring nun?

She tried to laugh. The smile she managed was more wistful than skeptical.

Her watch, still on European time, showed four in the morning. If one traveled only westward, would a day stretch into a week, a week into a month, and would she never emerge from her departure date? It seemed a hectic sort of immortality. In any case, it was tomorrow in Paris, and that was more than motive enough to take herself to bed.

"You mean you got in last night and didn't call? Vera, we would have picked you up. I'm frantic to hear about Katy."

"Katy is fine."

"I can't get through to her by phone."

"She's in Innsbruck. Austria. Skiing."

"I'm losing my mind and she's skiing?"

"Are you free for lunch?"

"You want lunch, I'll make you lunch. Come here."

Of course Dolores would think that the whole point of her trip had been to see Katy. After all, that had been the excuse. It was silly to assume that just because Vera knew there was no longer anything to worry about, Dolores, too, would know her daughter was okay.

"Is she putting on weight?"

"She'll be able to lose it."

"Lose it?" Dolores's eyes lifted. "I used to be able to lose weight. How do *you* keep so thin?"

"Prayer and fasting."

"Why should I get all the bad genes?"

Vera laughed. Her sister reminded her of their parents, combining the best traits of the two genetic lines. She was attractive in a sort of helter-skelter way, she was bright, she was loads of fun to be with. So what if she was a little chubby? Most good cooks are. And she sure was a good mother.

"A seminarian?" Dolores cried when Vera told the story. "He wants to be a priest?"

"It doesn't matter. It's all over."

"Just like that? She's so depressed she cries on the transatlantic phone, and now it's over? What did you say to her?"

It was flattering to think that she had solved her niece's problem. Maybe she had, in a way, by telling Ken what had happened to her marriage.

"I described Katy's parents. That scared him off."

"Funny."

"That's what he said."

"It's really all over?"

"Katy is happy as a lark. She is having the time of her life."

"Do you know what it costs us to have her spend her junior year in Rome? She better have a good time. What is her residence like?"

Dolores would settle for nothing less than the most detailed account of every meeting, every conversation, the restaurants, what Katy was wearing. And she wanted to hear about Ken, whom she called the rainmaker. She held her coffee cup in both hands and frowned into Vera's face as she talked.

"He doesn't sound like someone who would interest Katy."

"Maybe he wouldn't have, here in Chicago."

"I'll be glad when she's home."

"So you can pick her friends?"

"Ha!"

Dolores began to clear away the dishes. She banged the woven place mats on the edge of the sink, then dealt them back onto the table.

"So what else did you do?"

"A little sightseeing."

"Did you go to Paris?"

"Uh-huh."

Dolores returned to the chair across from Vera. "I would not have the guts to go to Paris alone."

"I didn't, the first time."

"I mean anytime. Can you imagine me saying something in French?"

"Easily."

"Did you meet some wonderful man?" Dolores made her brows dance comically.

"Oh, sure."

"Vera, you should have an affair. I mean that."

"Dolores! You'd better stop watching the soaps."

"Will you be hearing from whatchamacallit?"

"His name is Edward. And the answer is no."

"He telephoned here while you were gone. Wanted to know where you were."

"What did you tell him?"

"Howard answered. I would have hung up on him. I still think you should have taken all his money."

"What did Howard tell him?"

"That you were in Europe."

"He already knew that."

"Oh? Do you check in with him when you leave?"

"Dolores, we are not enemies. We lived together for over ten years. I cannot cancel that or pretend he doesn't exist."

"You should meet other men. You're young."

"And I'm married."

Dolores opened and closed her mouth. She knew that the sacrament of marriage was not dissolved by a divorce decree. While Edward lived, Vera was married to him and that was that.

"Get an annulment."

It was mildly tempting to tell Dolores that Edward had already tried that. "You should tell me to enter the convent, not to look for another man."

"The convent!" Dolores snorted. She had the happily married woman's healthy contempt for the life of the nun. "Sure, why not. You can take Jezebel's place."

"I think I'd make a good nun."

"Well, Edward made a bad one."

"Dolores!"

5.

In Paris she had walked in off an ordinary street to find a chapel where the Blessed Virgin Mary had appeared to Saint Catherine Laboure, who was buried right there, and where the heart of Saint Vincent de Paul was on display in a reliquary on a side altar. And where Mary had given Catherine the medal called miraculous. "Mary conceived without sin, pray for us who have recourse to you." That was the legend on its borders, surrounding the image of the Virgin.

The miraculous medal. There were plaques in the chapel commemorating the answers to petitions, miraculous cures, reunions, conversions. Kneeling there Vera had tried to feel repelled, but why should she so easily discard the common beliefs of Western civilization? It was false to think that these were things of the past, overcome by what we now know. Vera asked herself what she knew that prevented God from intervening in the affairs of men.

Faith continued; churches filled and emptied and filled again. Paul Claudel had been converted one Christmas Eve in Notre Dame and for the rest of his life remembered the hour, the place, the very pillar in the choir next to which he had stood. Vera read all about it in *Le Figaro*.

And she saw the crowds in the chapel on the rue de Bac, Frenchmen and foreigners, young and old, poor and rich, a cross-section of humanity. What did she know that they did not? It was what they knew that she craved to learn.

Home in Chicago she got out the phone book and found to her surprise that there was a Carmelite convent in Des Plaines. It seemed incredible that she could get in her car here in Chicago and go to what she had been unable to see in France, but in France it had been the Carmel where Sainte Thérèse had lived and died. What on earth would the Carmel of Des Plaines be?

It was an unprepossessing building set back from one corner of an intersection of highways, reached by a drive that circled in front of the entrance, its grounds in need of more trees. The place looked brand new.

Vera drove by and, a mile past, turned to come back. She went through the intersection three times before turning onto the gravel road. There were two cars parked in front of the entrance, so she felt less an intruder. She drew up behind the second, which had Wisconsin plates, shifted to neutral, and leaned across the passenger seat to study the building. To her right was a building she thought must be the chapel. It was some distance from the main door, so it would not be possible for her to look into it unannounced.

She had no idea what to do. Knock on the door? But what would she give as the purpose of her call? To see the chapel. Why not? The door opened then, and a priest appeared. He stood for a moment, speaking to a nun behind him. Vera strained to get a look, but the nun was in shadow. Then the priest was coming down the walk. Vera got out of her car before he could get into the one with Wisconsin plates.

"Father," she called, and he looked at her, squinting against the sun. Vera walked the few steps that separated them.

"This is a Carmelite convent, isn't it?"

"Yes, it is."

"Is there any way I can get inside?"

"Well, you could join." Regular teeth in a full face, eyes still invisible in their squint.

"I thought I'd look it over first."

"Good idea. I'm Father Collins." He looked at his watch. "I have to get back to Milwaukee." He hesitated a moment more. "Come on, I'll introduce you. What's your name?"

She told him as he started back up the walk, his open topcoat flapping around him, his black loafers flashing in the sunlight. Of course he was in full clerical dress. Vera realized she was not even surprised by this.

"You from Chicago?"

"That's right. I had no idea there was a Carmelite convent within a thousand miles."

"Thank God there is. When I was on the flake, these nuns prayed for me. God knows where or what I would be if it weren't for them."

They had reached the door, and he pressed a bell. It was then that Vera noticed the grille beside the door. A bodiless voice wished them good afternoon.

"Sister, this is Father Collins again. There is a woman here who would like to see the chapel. Okay?"

"Just a moment."

He waited with her until the door opened, so that she was thanking and saying good-bye to him at the same moment she looked for the first time into the serene face of a religious of the Order of Our Lady of Mount Carmel.

"Come in."

"Sister, I'm just a sightseer. I don't want to be a nuisance, but I would very much like to see the convent."

Father Collins, disappearing down the walk, waved as the door shut, and Vera turned to find herself in a hallway two stories high with a massive banner hanging from its ceiling. To the left was an open stairway leading to a balcony that traversed the hall.

"I am Sister Josephine," the nun said. "I will show you the chapel."

They reached it by going up the stairs and through a hall where there were small visiting rooms. Then, for the first time, Vera entered the chapel where, during the coming weeks, she would hear daily Mass.

She was inside perhaps half an hour. She was ready to be overwhelmed, but what she did was simply register external impressions. The brightness of the chapel, the prie-dieux where visitors knelt during Mass, an altar that while centered in the sanctuary faced away from the body of the chapel. The lectern, too, faced the back wall, and then Vera noticed the strangeness of that wall.

"That is the cloister," Sister Josephine said. She had genuflected reverently when they came into the chapel, but she spoke now in a normal voice. "It is opened during Mass so that the community can follow."

"Ah."

"As porter I must come out of the cloister, but the rest of the sisters never do."

In that place it seemed the most natural thing in the world. Sister Josephine's tone did not suggest anything extraordinary about the fact that a community of women had sealed themselves off from the world to live in cloistered isolation at an intersection in Des Plaines, Illinois.

Sister Josephine told her that she was welcome to come to Mass. Almost as decisive as that information was the pamphlet she gave Vera when they had returned to the front door.

It was a brief account of the life of Edith Stein, who, as Sister Teresa Benedicta of the Cross, had been put to death in Auschwitz. Vera was struck by the age at which Edith Stein entered Carmel. The date had been October 14, 1933. The place, the Carmel in Cologne. The age of the brilliant philosopher when she became a Carmelite was forty-two.

PART SIX

Todo y Nada

I.

Alma called to say she wanted to talk and to ask if it was okay for her to come out. Thank God she had telephoned first. Thank God she didn't just show up on the doorstep in Oak Park.

"Why don't we meet somewhere?" Andrea asked.

"Where?"

"You name a place."

"You." Alma's voice had been barely under control, and now she was almost inaudible.

"Where are you?"

Unmistakable sounds of crying, heartrending. Andrea put her hand over the mouthpiece as if that would still Alma's sobs. She spoke through her fingers, telling Alma she would meet her at Water Tower Place at 12:30. It was then ten in the morning.

"Do you understand? Water Tower. Twelve-thirty. Where are you now?" Listening to the muffled crying, Andrea felt pulled between impatience and compassion. "Alma, where are you?"

"A motel."

A motel! "Where? Where is it?"

"I'm not sure."

"Is Chuck with you?"

"Nooo!"

The motel was on Lake Shore Drive, south of the Loop, and Alma had no satisfying explanation for why she was there. It was somewhere away from Chuck, and that was enough. They had had a fight. Andrea felt no inclination to smile.

"I don't want to go to Water Tower," Alma wailed, and Andrea assured her that she could just stay where she was.

"I'll come there, Alma."

"When?"

"I'll be there as soon as I can."

It was called the Flamingo, a low, el-shaped structure, pink stucco, with overhanging eaves shadowing the fading pastel-colored doors of the units. There were two cars nuzzled up to numbered doors, one of them Chuck's, which explained how Alma had gotten there. Perhaps at night, bathed in merciful neon, the Flamingo had not looked so tacky, but in the sunless light of midmorning, it did not have the appeal of even a temporary haven. Andrea's first knock was timid, lest she alert the world, but after a minute she pounded on the cracked beige panel until she heard Alma's voice within.

"I was in the bathroom," Alma said when she swung the door open and blinked out at Andrea. The room behind her was dark and airless. Andrea searched for and found the drape cord and pulled the room into light. Alma watched her with the expression of a little lost girl. Their eyes met, Alma's lips trembled, and she burst into tears. Andrea took her in her arms and held her close until the worst was over.

"Get dressed, Alma. Let's get out of here."

"And go where?"

"Anywhere. How in the world did you end up here?"

Alma collapsed on the edge of the bed and looked around the room. "What's wrong with it?"

"Have you paid your bill?"

"I had to before they'd let me in."

"All right. Wash, dress, and we'll get out of here."

Even with the drapes opened and weak daylight illuminating the room, Alma acted as if she wanted nothing more than to stay there, to hide, to be consoled. It was important to be firm, and Andrea was firm. She did not want Alma clinging to her like a surrogate mother. Or a mother superior.

While she waited for Alma to finish in the bathroom, Andrea sat in an uncomfortable chair and looked at the featureless room. Unit. There would be identical units on either side, the same laminated furniture, the same headboard, similar nonpaintings hanging on the walls. Sometimes there seemed to be only the thinnest of lines between the world and the convent. The convents that used to be, anyway, the communities she and Alma had joined with their ordered, regulated days, and the sense one had of purpose and meaning in every trivial act. And all the rooms alike.

Andrea opened her purse to take out a cigarette, but instead of lighting it she just rolled it between her fingers, staring at it. Her new habit. What had brought her to it? What had brought Alma to this depressing motel unit? An argument with Chuck, it appeared, but what had brought her to Chuck? Chuck had been taken on at a bank, recommended by another laicized priest, and it was a mindless, ill-paying job. The longed-for freedom had turned into a deeper boredom and disappointment. Andrea thought of Edward.

She did not really want to get more involved than she was, and this frantic call from Alma, the dim epiphany of the motel unit, confirmed her judgment. She did not want her life to escape her control, or to become dependent on the whim of another. Her relationship with Edward was what it was. Such satisfaction—triumph?—as it had involved was, if not gone, then familiar enough to have lost its charm.

"We can get married by a judge, if you want."

She had smiled tolerantly. Why did Edward seem so like a little boy now? "Edward, what is the point? I am not likely to have children."

That had made him very angry and even more like a little boy. What she had thought of as a simple observation had wounded his vanity.

He said, "You sound like Vera."

Aha. "Would you like to make a baby?"

He was gentle; she never failed to be surprised at how gentle he was. She had half expected to be overwhelmed by physical strength, but he could not have been more tender.

Before they left the Flamingo Motel, they had to discuss Chuck Rupert's car, parked outside the unit. To leave it there would be like abandoning it. Andrea suggested parking it in a lot in the Loop and informing Chuck.

"I don't want to talk to him."

"You won't have to."

They left it at McCormack Place. Poor Chuck. It would cost him a fortune to redeem his car, even if he came for it that day.

When Alma slid into the passenger seat beside Andrea, she was almost cheerful.

"I am so glad we got away from that motel."

"When did you go there?"

"What day is today?"

"What *day!* It's Tuesday."

"Sunday night."

"Two days ago? I thought you hadn't left the place since you checked in."

"I didn't."

"You haven't eaten?"

"Oh, I ate. There were pop and junk food dispensers by the ice machine."

At Water Tower Place they spent over an hour riding escalators, looking into shops and boutiques, browsing in Rizzoli's and ended up, because Alma liked it, in a cutesy little place with a view of the inevitable fountain, having quiche Lorraine and white wine.

"I should think you'd want something more substantial."

Alma rolled her eyes, squeezed them shut, stuck her tongue out one side of her mouth and then the other. "This is exactly what I wanted."

"Let's have another glass of wine."

"Okay."

"And you can tell me what happened."

What happened was what always happened, and Alma just couldn't stand it anymore. "The man is an animal," she said, keeping her voice now, pronouncing each word very distinctly. "An animal. I had no idea he was like that. All those years of celibacy, and it's as if he has to make up for everything he missed." She dropped her voice and again spoke as if for lip-readers. "Every single night. Every morning, too, if I didn't get into the shower fast before he woke up. I feel like I'm in prison."

The indoor-outdoor scene beyond their table held the eye—cascading fountain, full-size trees rising between the floors, shoppers looking down and up at one another, a skylight high above, and beyond that, presumably, something God and not man had made. Andrea listened as if to her own fears, fears that had not quite been realized with Edward.

"Lying in that motel I developed a theory. We are ruined for normal life, Andrea."

"Don't generalize so quickly."

"Name me a happily married ex-priest or ex-nun."

"I haven't made a survey."

"Just name one."

"Who was the nun Martin Luther married?"

"Did he marry a nun?"

"He did. And he was a priest."

It was absurd for Alma to pretend she had not known that. Best to be blunt.

"Have you decided to leave him?"

Wide, vulnerable eyes. "Why not? I left the convent; I guess I can leave a husband. That is the point of my theory. We're ruined for permanent relations."

Andrea did not like that "we." Thank God Alma did not know about Edward. Or, at least, did not know all there was to know. When Edward had first shown real interest in her, Andrea had confided in Alma, and they had giggled a bit like school girls over it. And gone on to commiserate with all wives whose husbands, even the best, would take any chance to wander.

"Tell me why you left him."

"What do you mean?"

"Why did you go to that motel? Did you argue first, or what? Does he know you're gone?"

"He knows now."

She had left while he was watching a baseball game on television, ostensibly to go to the store; he had distractedly registered her explanation as she went out the door. The prospect that lay ahead, with the coming of night and the end of the game, was suddenly more than Alma could bear. She felt trapped and suffocated.

"He brought home manuals, illustrated. Andrea, I left him in front of the set and went into the kitchen and nearly passed out when I had an image of what my life used to be like. When I was first in, a novice, the year afterward. Dear God, the peace I felt."

And no doubt Chuck missed the bachelor calm of the rectory, where he could watch a ball game without feeling he was neglecting someone. But Andrea did not really want to adopt an evenhanded view, see Chuck's side of it. Alma viewed her plight in terms Andrea could not avoid applying to herself.

"Alma, it no longer exists. You couldn't go back to it even if you wanted to."

"Why was it destroyed?"

There were answers to that, almost too many answers, but how unconvincing they would have seemed if she had voiced them there in the mall within earshot of the splashing fountain, seated at the little wrought iron table with its snowy linen, sipping wine, enjoying a cigarette.

"It's not our fault, Alma. We didn't make all the changes."

"We didn't stop them either."

Andrea did not say that she had tried. At first. In any case, she had supported those who tried.

"I thought lots of things all alone in that motel. I thought, why not see how many nuns would like to go back to the life we lost, women from different orders; that wouldn't matter. And we wouldn't need permission; it wouldn't have to be official. We could just live together in the old way, and that would be it."

"Supporting yourselves?"

"No. No jobs. We would stay there, not go out."

"And wear habits?"

"Yes! Honestly, I wouldn't mind going back to that. I would *like* it. How about you, Andrea?"

"Let's just say I understand your feeling."

"Please don't *explain* me. I am so tired of being explained. That's when everything began to fall apart, when we began to explain ourselves."

"I didn't mean it like that."

"When I entered, there was no talk of finding yourself or getting in touch with yourself or any of that. There was this ideal and I was to spend my life trying to live up to it and that was that."

Andrea just let her talk. It was a safe place for that; the strangers going by kept Alma under control, and she babbled on, voicing all the thoughts she had had while cooped up in that creepy motel. Andrea ordered yet

another glass of wine, but Alma was exhilarated enough
with her dream of returning to a no-longer-existent past.

"And what will you call your order?"

"I want you in it, Andrea."

"Thank you."

"We weren't meant for this. You know we weren't. I
hate trying to be like other women. God didn't mean
for us to be like other women."

It was the first time Alma had mentioned God in
discussing her ideas. How could Andrea avoid thinking
that, for Alma, and for many others, it was not the
religious aspect of the religious life that appealed but
its security, its predictability, its routine. The routine
had involved a lot of prayer, common and private, but
what had really mattered was the community, living
with these women, sheltered from the world.

"Poverty, chastity, obedience."

Alma repeated the names of the vows, relishing the
words and their associations. She leaned toward Andrea.

"I felt so clean then."

2.

Twice Vera drove to Milwaukee to see Father
Collins, once she met him at the Carmel of Des Plaines.
He was delighted at her interest in Edith Stein, particularly when he learned that Vera's undergraduate
major had been philosophy.

"Where?"

"St. Catherine's."

"A woman's college. Well, Edith taught young women and spent a lot of time studying Aquinas after she came into the Church. But she was trained as a phenomenologist." When Vera frowned in incomprehension, he said, "The same as the pope."

He spoke of *The Science of the Cross,* the Jewish nun's book on Saint John of the Cross, and then Teresa of Ávila, *The Interior Castle.* For the first time Vera felt she had some intimation of what the saints meant by prayer.

"I think a picture with my eyes closed and then just sit there."

Father Collins nodded. He seemed to be listening to something inaudible to her. Doubtless her newfound enthusiasm bored him.

"No." He shook his head. "No. I know what you're going through. Discovering the wheel. We were taught it all as kids, and we threw it away. I got a second chance because the nuns here read of some stupid remarks I had made about the Church and put me on their list. They prayed me back. I was on the flake, and they prayed me back. Why did I get a second chance? Why did you?"

"Is there an answer?"

"Not that I know of."

She attended Mass in the chapel, arriving early so she could hear the cloister screen slide back and try to catch a glimpse of the nuns behind the grille. The secrecy of their lives, although they lived in an intersection in Des Plaines—perhaps because of that—fascinated Vera, and her fascination was fed by reading of Edith Stein as well as of the Little Flower.

"I tried to get to Lisieux once."

Father Collins nodded. "What do you mean you *were* married?"

"My husband left me. He tried to get an annulment. Then he got a divorce."

"In order to marry again?"

"Yes."

"Was the marriage valid?"

The question offended her, much as Edward's effort to get an annulment had.

"The reason I ask, don't get your hopes up about ending up in a place like this."

"Me? Here?"

Her attempted laugh sounded more like a sob.

"Elizabeth Seton now, she was a widow. That's different."

"Edward is very much alive."

"That's my point."

Talking with him lost its edge after that. How had he guessed? But what else would he have thought, for heaven's sake, a middle-aged woman showing such curiosity about a convent. It was silly. Did she want to dress up, was that it?

"There are still third orders, you know."

She listened to him talk, but the kind of tenuous connection with Franciscans and Dominicans and Benedictines offered to laypeople by third order membership seemed a mockery of the hope she had been nurturing. How ironic that she had taken Edith Stein as a model. Edith Stein had had to wait ten years before she was permitted to enter the Carmel of Cologne.

·   ·   ·

I look at Him and He looks at me. That is how Saint Jean Vianney, the Curé d'Ars, explained his way of praying. Things came easily when Vera stopped trying. The books she read made it sound like an intricate skill to be mastered only with practice. Books on mental prayer bore a strange relation to the books on sex she and Edward had sheepishly read in the hope of learning the trick of fecundity.

Sacrilegious? Not really. The basic metaphor of the spiritual life was the bridegroom and the bride, the soul receiving Christ as lover. Vera remembered how repelled she had been when Andrea told her that the nun is called the Bride of Christ. Now she was repelled by the thought of being the bride of Edward.

No, not repelled. But it was no longer painful to recall the fact that he had left her. To be abandoned. To be treated unjustly. To be betrayed as she had been by both Edward and Andrea. Was it really all that bad? In a way these were blessings. She traced upon her body the sign of the Cross, and that meant acceptance of Jesus, a willingness to live as he had lived. It was when she thought of herself and Jesus as fellow losers that she was able to sit still, shut out thoughts and images, and simply be together with God.

"I thought for a while of entering the Trappists, as a penance." A little smile came and went on Father Collins's face.

"What changed your mind?"

"Visiting a Trappist abbey. I made a retreat, at least I started one, but I left before forty-eight hours were up." His moonlike face was pocked; his eyes perpetually squinted. "Listen to me. Criticizing the Trappists. But it was a silly retreat. The director took his texts from Joan Baez lyrics. For this I have to go to a Trappist abbey?"

"Don't they keep perpetual silence?"

"Not anymore. It's not at all like it used to be. Don't misunderstand, it is still a very demanding life, but it has not been left unscathed by all the changes in the Church."

He had thought of the Carthusians, too. There was a house in this country, but he flew to England to look them over.

"They are still the real article. A mixture of cenobitic and hermetic life." He did not explain. Vera would have looked up the words if she could have imagined how they were spelled.

"Did you ask to be admitted?"

He squeezed his eyes shut, then looked over her head. "My English was so different from theirs. For the rest of my life I would have sounded like a comedian whenever I spoke. Good for humility, maybe, but I couldn't face it. I think of all that as a temptation now."

"I don't understand."

"For me, anyway, thinking of a monastic life is self-indulgent. I already have a vocation. It's too easy to think I would be automatically better in another life. I am sure I wouldn't be. Don't get caught in romantic dreams of the religious life, Vera."

Edward came to see her at the office, and it was impossible not to think of their first meeting. He was incapable of looking after his own financial affairs and wanted professional help.

"Young Conboy is very good."

"Why don't you do it, Vera? I don't want some stranger prying into my private affairs."

"Are you sure you want me to be privy to them?"

"You already are."

"It would be a conflict of interest situation, Edward."

"How so?" He looked at her blankly.

"We were married." She lowered her voice, and he leaned forward to hear. Almost immediately he pulled back. Vera felt she had told a dirty joke.

"You already know all there is to know."

"That doesn't matter."

"Maybe I shouldn't have gotten a divorce."

This seemed to be what he had come to tell her. Their eyes met across her desk. His expression was the silly boyish one he wore when he wanted something very much. Vindication, triumph, a desire to punish him? Vera felt none of these. She felt that she was being betrayed a second time.

3.

Alma had spoken more wisely than she knew, or at any rate than Andrea had suspected, when she said they were incapable of living like ordinary women. You can take the girl out of the convent . . . It was amazing how similar their lives had been, despite belonging to different orders.

On the other hand, maybe no woman could have lived with Chuck Rupert.

He came to Andrea in his effort to get Alma to come back to him, waylaying her when she got out of her car in front of the apartment. How long had he been waiting there?

He looked at his watch, then shrugged away the question as an irrelevancy.

"Can we talk?" His eyes drifted toward the apartment. Andrea imagined Alma up there, peeking out at her husband, dreading having to face him.

"Buy me a drink."

Chuck brightened at the suggestion, hope softening his haunted look.

The suggestion of a drink had seemed right at the time, but when they were settled into a booth at the proletarian bar on the other side of the freeway, Andrea saw that Chuck had already been drinking. He ordered a glass of beer and a shot of whiskey; it might have been the *specialité de la maison*. Andrea would never have come into such a bar alone. Was it any better to have come here with Chuck? She asked for a Diet Coke.

"Why won't she talk to me, Andrea? She's my wife."

"Chuck, please don't put me in the middle."

"Aren't you a counselor?"

"I am also Alma's friend. And yours," she added. "I can't be objective."

Had he even heard what she said? "She can't leave me. Do you know what it meant to me, to stop being a priest? That was my life, and I threw it aside for Alma."

"Maybe you should go back."

"Back?"

"Men return to the priesthood after . . ." She could think of no euphemism to cover his marriage to Alma.

Why did it embarrass her to think of Alma with this man? Stories of Chuck's sexual appetite had affected her attitude toward him, no doubt of that. Alma had called him an animal. Andrea sipped her Coke.

"I can't go back."

"Why not?"

"I don't want to go back. I want Alma."

Improbable Romeo, overweight and weak, was it possible that he loved Alma, really loved her? Her own experience with Edward had made Andrea skeptical of men. Desire dictated protestations of love and devotion, but desire once satisfied wiped the slate clean again. Was it love or remembered sex that had brought Chuck to their doorstep, teary-eyed, lips atremble, drunk? And he was drunk. There was little doubt of that.

"In the seminary we called those who left quitters. It was important to hang in there, get ordained. Those who got laicized later were treated better than quitters. But they were still failures." He moved his shot glass around the damp surface of the table, but his eyes were on the cloudy window that obscured the street. God knew what trumped-up memories he saw there. "I don't want to fail twice."

"Twice?"

"First as a priest, then as a husband. What am I good for?"

"You're still a priest, Chuck."

He shuddered at the reminder. Thou art a priest forever. It was a condemnation, not a consolation. But he had never been laicized. He and Alma had just married. It wasn't even a marriage the Church would recognize, a civil ceremony, a paper transaction. Why had they bothered? Neither of them really believed in the efficacy of that certificate.

Andrea could imagine how Chuck felt. A failed priest, now a failed husband, what confidence could he have left in himself? Thank God she had had the sense to keep from becoming permanently entangled with Edward. An exhilarating flight in a rented plane, dalliance on the *Dental Flaws*, the odd feeling that she had become for a time Vera, ceased being herself. But she could regain her own identity, and she had. The thought formed easily: let Edward go back to Vera.

Andrea was sure that he would.

Let Chuck go back to the priesthood. Would not the archdiocese rejoice even more in the return of one lost shepherd than in the hundreds who had stayed on the job? Of course it would. People like Chuck were said to have been on leave of absence. Perhaps he had caused some public scandal, but scandal was not what it used to be. Laypeople no longer expected very much of priests. Or of nuns, for that matter.

"Will you talk to Alma?"

"Chuck, it would be better just to leave her alone for a while. Let things cool down."

"Why did she leave me?" He was really puzzled. Well, it was unlikely he would regard himself as an animal.

"She probably doesn't know herself."

Strange that such a remark should comfort him, but it did. He ordered another beer, no shot this time.

"I don't want to see him again. Ever."

"Then you don't have to."

Alma tightened her embrace. "What did he say?"

"He wants you back."

"What did you tell him?"

"Alma, it doesn't matter. He was half-drunk."

With Edward, Andrea had felt like a substitute for Vera. Holding Alma she felt she was standing in for Chuck. When was she acting for herself?

4.

Vera stopped going to the Carmelite convent for Mass, and it was a penance not doing penance anymore.

What was the nature of her attachment to the place, to its atmosphere, to the prayers she managed to say when time seemed a footnote to eternity? She felt closer to God now, but the closeness wasn't tied to a particular place. Among the things she'd been reading at home were the poems of Emily Dickinson. She had never realized before how intensely religious, in a New England sort of way, the poet had been.

And people were always dying in her poems. Death was almost attractive in those swiftly written lines, so uneven in accomplishment, so repetitive in theme, so wonderful.

> The silence condescended—
> Creation stopped—for Me—
> But awed beyond my errand—
> I worshipped—did not 'pray'

Was it any sillier to feel affinity for the Maid of Amherst than to dream of being a nun after all her years of marriage? Father Collins had guessed her secret. She had told no one else. Until, kiddingly, when describing the Carmelite convent for Dolores, she had said she might as well enter now that Edward had left her.

"Is he going to marry Andrea?"

"That's the idea."

"His? Hers? Both?"

"You sound like you know something."

Dolores pushed the sleeves of her sweater up her arms, then pulled them down again. "He came to see Howard. At the office."

"No."

"Vera, he wants to come back to you, and he thought Howard would take his side. Don't you let him. I'd rather see you join the convent than go back to that sonofabitch." Dolores could feel strong emotions only on behalf of others—concern for Katy, indignation for Vera. At the moment she looked as if she'd like to strangle Edward.

"Married women can't become nuns."

"Would you let him come back?"

"No."

A single syllable, a slight disturbance of air, a tone of resolution. Did she mean it? Vera did not want to think it mattered. Edward would not come back; he would not want to come back. Andrea or someone else, he would find a woman to mother him, and that was all he wanted.

And why shouldn't it be Andrea?

Vera thought of the odd explanation that Ken the seminarian had offered in Rome, and she smiled. Andrea had been straight as an arrow as a girl, and even now her affair or whatever it was with Edward was theoretical, an experiment. What made Ken's remark semi-plausible was Andrea's feminism.

Vera had been exempted from her harangues—why tell a lady lawyer she was the victim of male oppression? —but snatches of her rhetoric had drifted across the room, across the deck of the *Dental Flaws,* as Andrea orated to Edward.

Had that been a mode of seduction, convincing Edward that he along with other males had taken unjust advantage of Andrea and all other women? By conferring honorary oppressor status on Edward, Andrea had linked him to herself, almost as if they had sinned together. Vera, who for years had longed for motherhood and the chance to stay home and raise a family, was unreceptive to such talk. But then Andrea's feminism had a distinctively churchy cast.

"Why haven't women been ordained?" she demanded of an apparently interested Edward.

"Why haven't men become nuns?"

She hit his arm. "I'm serious. The structures of the Church are paternalistic. They always have been. There is a built-in contempt for women in the Catholic Church."

Hadn't the charge once been Mariolatry? Vera had no views on the matter. Let Andrea be a priestess if she wanted. But why did she want to be one?

"Power. The real power is clerical. Until women have it . . ."

Vera tuned it out. The politicization of religion, that was what Andrea's feminism had meant.

And then, after Edward's revelation, after the trip to

Europe, when Vera got some inkling of what Andrea's lifelong religious vocation had meant, she could not understand what Andrea felt deprived of. There was only one power worth having, from a religious point of view, and everyone already had it.

Let us put ourselves in the presence of God.

It was hard not to conjecture now what Andrea's prayer had been like. Had she had any? Had she lived all those years close to God and nonetheless slipped into bed with Edward out of mere curiosity? It was spooky to think that years and years of living one way could be so easily set aside. Vera still did not think that anything like love had been involved. Not on Andrea's side, anyway.

5.

"We have to talk," Andrea said on the phone, urgency in her voice.

"I don't think so."

"Vera, it's not just about Edward."

"There's nothing to talk about."

But there was, of course. There was a topic that was unlikely to come up. Vera would have liked to ask Andrea what it was like to be a nun. Now at last she wanted to talk to her about the things that, in long-ago letters, had seemed so unintelligible. Once Andrea had feared that all women would enter the convent if they knew how wonderful it was, and Vera had wondered why any woman would. In a funny way Edward had become a link between them, permitting them to exchange roles. Take my husband, please. And I'll get me to a nunnery.

Andrea's dress looked to be denim but up close proved to be brushed velvet. Her hair was parted in the middle and hung to her shoulders. Her face was thin, too thin, and there was a haunted look in her eyes.

"Chuck is dead."

"Chuck?"

"The man Alma married. Chuck Rupert. The priest. I told you about him."

Vera had no memory of it, but what did that matter? Alma the nun had married Chuck the priest. It made you want to scream or laugh or cry.

"What happened to him?"

"He committed suicide." The vestige of an old dread crept into Andrea's whisper. Vera did not remember ever having heard of Chuck. Did Andrea think of him now in hell, beyond mercy, guilty of despair? "I haven't told Alma that. She mustn't feel responsible for what he did."

"When did they get married?"

"It was just a civil thing."

"Alma was a nun?" Vera's image of the woman was of someone small, open-faced, vulnerable.

"Yes."

"Did she ever miss it, Andrea? The convent? Do you?"

"Some of my best memories are of the convent."

"Tell me about it."

"It would only bore you."

"You didn't think so when you wrote me about it."

"Did you keep my letters?"

"At the time they made no sense to me."

"At the time?"

"Maybe I would understand them now."

"There's very little to understand. It was like the Girl Scouts, Vera. First it was the habit, and then it was not wearing the habit. Mainly it was a sense of belonging to something. Solidarity. Sisters. A kind of sorority."

"That doesn't sound like your letters."

"Then I'm glad you didn't keep them."

They sat in Stouffer's. Vera had ordered tea, shades of Dayton's, but if Andrea remembered, she gave no sign of it. It was midafternoon, and the restaurant was all but empty. It was the first place to pop into Vera's mind when Andrea called her at the office. She had assumed this would be a heart-to-heart talk about Edward. The trick would be to keep Andrea from knowing how much she wanted her to take Edward. Whether or not the Carmelites would have her, she knew how she wanted to live her life. Edward now seemed a threat.

Andrea did talk of her life as a nun. At first it was a matter of sisterly solidarity. But very early on it became a matter of resentment. Religion as resentment. Nuns had been repressed by priests, women by men. The Church must finally come of age and recognize the role of women.

"First you wanted to be a nun. Now you want to be a priest?"

"No. Not anymore. I got over that, too."

"What do you mean?"

Andrea's narrow face was naturally ascetic, a Goya face. There were traces of eye shadow on her lids. Blink, blue, blink, blue. It might have been a signal. Perhaps it was.

A priest named Chuck was dead. She could not discern Andrea's reaction. Her concern was for her friend, Alma, former nun, now widow.

"She's under sedation."

"You should be with her."

"Yes. That's the point of this conversation. Vera, about Edward."

Her incredible message was that she was returning Vera's husband to her. Her duty lay with Alma.

"It was never really serious, Vera."

"Adultery seldom is."

"I wouldn't know."

Was she suggesting that she had never slept with Edward? That was not it. Rather, Andrea wished to be thought of as relatively innocent, guilty of only one lapse. It seemed curiously fastidious of her.

"Edward has already spoken to me."

"What do you mean?"

"He has gotten word to me that it's all over between you. He spoke to Dolores's husband."

"When?"

Of course she had expected, hoped for, Andrea's reaction. Andrea had to understand she no longer had an Edward to give back to his rightful spouse.

"Will you take him back, Vera?"

"I don't see why I should."

Andrea began to say something, then stopped. The

silence that ensued was set against a background of tinkling silverware and the murmur of voices from the few others there. Andrea put her hand on Vera's.

"Still friends?"

The incredible is best met with a smile. Vera looked across the table at her old friend and enemy. Once she had seen that face framed in the headdress of a religious habit. It all seemed so long ago.

The oars dipped into the waters of Belmont Harbor as Edward rowed them out to the *Dental Flaws*. What was the name of the ship on which the Japanese had surrendered to MacArthur? The sky was slate gray; there was a threat of rain. In trying to get aboard, Vera lost her footing, but Edward boosted her up before she fell. That minor ignominy caused her to hang on to a guy wire even after she took a seat on deck. Edward went below and unlocked the cabin. The *Dental Flaws* rocked rhythmically with the harbor tide. It seemed a fitting place for reconciliation.

Vera wore white slacks, sneakers, a nylon jacket. She shivered at a coldness that had little to do with the temperature. Swaying with the water, she felt that her dreams of a life of prayer had been stolen from her, by Edward, by Andrea, by the priest who had committed suicide, by Alma. Beneath her the boat rolled gently. *Out of the cradle, endlessly rocking.* She would never have children. In that at least she would be like a nun.

Edward sat down beside her. For a while he said nothing. Above them a gull landed on the mast, making an unoiled, unmusical sound.

"It was my fault," Edward said.

"That's all right."

He hugged his knees and looked at Chicago as if it were some strange landscape he did not recognize.

"I mean about children."

She said nothing.

He said, "I'm sterile."

God only knew what courage it took for him to say that. His voice sounded tinny and odd, and he looked away from her.

"I went to a doctor," he said. "I had tests made."

"So did I."

He did not seem to have heard her. "He took tests and told me I was sterile. We could never have children." He took a deep breath and drew a package of cigarettes from his pocket, looked at them, then threw them onto the deck. "Even if you had been able to, I couldn't have."

She let it go. Poor Edward. They had linked their lives once and for all, for better or worse, and it did no good to kick against the goad. He had tried to escape and failed. Isn't that what she herself had been attempting, escape of another sort? Perhaps. It was strange to think of God as a temptation. But then, she couldn't escape from God. What she wanted was not confined to one place, in another country, away from Edward.

"Did you really want to be a nun?"

"Who told you that?"

"Howard."

"He was repeating a joke of Dolores's."

He picked up the cigarettes and removed one from the package. She lit it for him, using the lighter she found in his pocket. How acrid the smoke smelled. He looked at her as the smoke trailed from his mouth and was borne away in the wind.

"Some joke."

"A married woman can't become a nun, Edward."

She did not see Andrea until a bitterly cold day in October. Stouffer's again. It could become a tradition. Maybe it was the weather, but Andrea looked older. Was she happy to learn that Vera and Edward were back together?

"Was it the loneliness, Vera? I don't blame you. No one can live alone."

"You do."

"No, I have Alma."

"Oh."

"Don't knock it."

"Knock, knock. Remember those jokes?"

Andrea pursed her lips and tossed her hair. "Who's there?"

"Peabody."

"Peabody who?"

"Peabody fence while nobody's looking."

It was better than talking of Edward. Or of Alma.

After she left Andrea, Vera walked toward St. Peter's, the downtown Franciscan church. The wind whipped at her, seeming to come from several directions at once. The spirit breathes where it will. Edward wanted to sell the *Dental Flaws* and get a larger boat. In the spring they would take a trip to Greece. Meanwhile Edward went on filling cavities, and Vera, a full partner now, gave expensive advice to clients.

Praying in St. Peter's was like praying in a train depot,

a constant coming and going of people. Presumably they came to pray. All kind of people pray all the time, and she had thought of it as unique. She wanted to be a saint, a heroine, someone like Edith Stein. But she had Edward and vice versa. She sat in a pew and closed her eyes, holding back the tears. Prayer is getting in touch with God. But what is God? *Todo y nada*, according to John of the Cross. Everything and nothing.

The Spanish was better.

Todo y nada.

RALPH MCINERNY has written ten novels, including *Connolly's Life* and *The Noonday Devil*, which find their themes in the groves of academe and the often comic, sometimes tragic, commotion that plagues the post-conciliar Church. He is also the author of two mystery series, one featuring the beloved Father Dowling and the other written pseudonymously as Monica Quill.

Since 1955 McInerny has taught at the University of Notre Dame, where he is Michael P. Grace Professor of Medieval Studies and Director of the Jacques Maritain Center.